The Scorpion's Bite

To Aiiste

Happy Reading

Aileen R. Baron

Books by Aileen G. Baron

A Fly Has a Thousand Eyes
The Torch of Tangier
The Gold of Thrace
The Scorpion's Bite

The Scorpion's Bite

A Lily Sampson Mystery

Aileen G. Baron

Poisoned Pen Press

Poisoned Pen Press

Copyright © 2010 by Aileen G. Baron

First Edition 2010

10 9 8 7 6 5 4 3 2

Library of Congress Catalog Card Number: 2009942214

ISBN: 9781590587539 Hardcover
9781590587553 Trade Paperback
9781615952519 Epub

Poisoned Pen Press
6962 E. First Ave., Ste. 103
Scottsdale, AZ 85251
www.poisonedpenpress.com
info@poisonedpenpress.com

Printed in the United States of America

To Nelson Glueck, master of the archaeological survey,
who could spot a microlith from the back of a camel,
and palm sheep's eyeballs with the best of them

Chapter One

The three of them sat in the shade of the Jeep, mouths dry, throats heavy with the scorching air, seared by relentless heat, huddled close, but still not completely sheltered from the unforgiving sun. They were almost out of water, just a few drops in their canteens and in the canvas bag hanging limp on the side of the Jeep.

They were in the Wadi Rum, stuck there with a broken axle: Lily, with Gideon Weil, director of the American School in Jerusalem, and their photographer, Klaus Steiner, doing an archaeological survey of Trans-Jordan for the OSS.

And Lily had no idea why.

Last March, more than three months after the Allies took North Africa in Operation Torch, General Donovan appeared in Casablanca looking for Lily Sampson. This time, she thought Wild Bill Donovan was going to tell her to go back south, past Marrakesh and Volubis, into sub-Saharan Africa. Instead, he sent her back to Jerusalem, told her to be ready in twenty-four hours. She was used to this from Donovan.

She left Morocco the next morning at ten o'clock, flying out of the Naval Airbase at Port Lyautey. She landed at Kolundia, the small airport north of Jerusalem, and took a taxi to the American School of Oriental Research where Gideon Weil, the director, was waiting for her.

Gideon had once been on the cover of *Time* magazine, in all the glory of his dark good looks and his roguish smile, sitting atop a camel like a Bedouin. He wore a *kafiya* with a dashing tilt.

He told her they were going to do an archaeological survey of Trans-Jordan. He had been working on the survey since before the war, had already published two volumes of research.

Klaus Steiner, a refugee from Hitler's Germany, caught up with them in Jericho. Steiner sported an ascot, a very British blond mustache, a scar on his left cheek, and a gold-capped canine tooth that glinted when he smiled. He told them he had been assigned to them as photographer.

The three of them crossed the Jordan at Allenby Bridge and spent the next month traipsing up and down the ancient King's Highway, visiting cities of the Roman Decapolis.

Lily felt superfluous.

They spent a week mapping Jerash, ancient Gerasa. It had been mapped before; it had been dug ten years ago.

In the midst of the ruins of Jerash, they passed a fellah with an ox and an ass yoked together and pulling a plow. Gideon pointed out that in Deuteronomy, it was forbidden to yoke them together like that. Klaus rolled his eyes to the sky in a show of impatience with Gideon quoting the Bible.

When they reached Amman, Gideon set Lily and Klaus to mapping and photographing remains of the well-documented Roman theater while he made a courtesy call on His Highness, Emir Abdullah.

That afternoon, Gideon told them they were going to Wadi Rum, then on to Petra to meet someone.

Now they sat stranded in the Wadi Rum where tall sandstone cliffs rear straight up like cathedrals, like castles of the mind. When they first reached Wadi Rum, they had stopped the Jeep and sucked in their breath, awed by its grandeur: the pink sand, the clean stillness in the air, the high, red cliffs, echoing silence.

"Red," Gideon had said. "The color of Edom is red, ruddy like Esau, the father of the Edomites, who sold his birthright to Jacob for a mess of red lentils," and Klaus rolled his eyes again.

Today was a lost cause. They had to stick to the track that ran through the wadi without a clue to the whereabouts of either archaeological sites or the Bedouin camps. They were looking for both.

Their Bedouin guide, Qasim, had vanished this morning and left them to fend for themselves.

Last night, as they had every night, they sat around the campfire in the cool desert air, breathing the perfume of the desert and the pungent odor of wormwood and tamarisk, watching the firelight flicker on Qasim's face as he told them tales of his family, of the tribe of the Howeitat, tales of raiding for sheep and camels, of noble gestures. They sat, warmed by the crackle of the fire, with sparks flying upward into the night of brilliant stars, and listened to his stories of how the greedy Saudis, craving power and drunk with religious fervor, raided his people, impoverished them, and how the British betrayed them and sided with the Saudis.

And all day long, Klaus was out with his camera, climbing the hills, vanishing into the fissures in the turreted limestone cliffs, coming back hours later telling them he had shots of rock drawings, or yet another magnificent vista of the clean, silent, wasteland of the desert.

Qasim was missing and the dapper Klaus—his eyebrows and lashes pointed with the red dust of the wadi, his moustache caked with pink powder—sat with them, grumbling about the heat and the rowdy wind, his camera wrapped in a towel.

All they could do was watch sand whirl in gusts as it piled against the small dune opposite the Jeep, gape at the overwhelming desert, and wait for help to come.

◇◇◇

A dark spot emerged above the crest of the horizon and Lily watched it approach from over the high ridge, seeming to erupt out of the hills beyond the blowing sand. She could just make out the figure moving toward them.

As the figure came closer, Lily saw that it was a child, a girl no more than eight or ten. She was dressed in adult finery with a small abayah over her long dress. A veil, sweeping in the wind, covered her head, a necklace of coins draped across her forehead.

She came toward them, her face engraved with the dry dust of the desert.

"Those Bedouin," Klaus said. "Where do they all come from? They're everywhere, coming out of nowhere in the desert, keeping an eye on us, watching our every move."

"Desert hospitality," Gideon said. "They're our hosts, we're their guests."

"And they'll invite us at knife point to sleep in their camps with their bedbugs and rotted cheese."

"It's all they have," Gideon said. "They share what they have, bedbugs and all."

The Bedouin girl carried a tiered tray, covered with a cloth against the dust. She set it down on the running board of the Jeep and removed the cloth, revealing three cups and a pot of tea. She poured the tea, gave them a shy smile, and sat silently on the small dune opposite the Jeep while they drank the tea and muttered, "*Shukran, shukran,*" to the girl between sips. "Thank you, thank you."

When they finished, the child, still silent, collected the cups, trudged back over the hill, and disappeared.

And they continued to wait, marooned in the wind and sand and desert pavement.

The wind picked up, blowing around them, the sound of it escalating like an eerie whine of spirits who had vanished in the Wadi Rum.

Lily peered down the wadi and saw a whirlwind roaring toward them, eddying over boulders, picking up rocks and branches of brush in its vortex as it advanced.

"Dust devil!" Gideon shouted over the noise of the wind.

Lily closed her eyes and covered her face with her scarf as the whirlwind came nearer still, swirling and biting into their skin, sputtering and roaring as it closed around them, trajectories of rock and sand stinging the bare flesh of her arms and hands.

She held her breath, struggled against the gritty air, drowned in sand.

Thirty seconds passed and she tried to breathe.

One minute—with wind snapping her clothes, howling in her ears.

Another minute, gasping.

Then the wind passed and traveled up the wadi.

They coughed, sipped from what was left in their canteens, and coughed again.

"Behold," Gideon said. "A storm of the Lord is gone forth in fury, yes a whirling storm."

"Not another." Klaus gave Gideon an impatient look before he snapped a picture of the disappearing whirlwind. "Not another Biblical quotation."

"It's from Jeremiah."

Klaus rewrapped the towel around his camera. "You are also a rabbi, yes?"

Gideon nodded. "My degree is in theology. My dissertation was on the meaning of *ahavah* in the Old Testament."

"And what is the meaning of *ahavah?*"

"Love," Lily said.

"You took a hundred and eighty-seven pages to say that?" Klaus asked.

Gideon looked over at him. "A hundred and eighty-seven pages? How do you know?"

"I saw in our library at university. Göttingen, no?"

"You told me you were at Heidelberg." Gideon ran a finger along his own cheek, approximating Klaus' scar. "With a dueling mark on your left cheek to prove it."

"You are mistaken." Klaus stood up. "Göttingen." He beat some of the grit off his pants, carefully unwrapped his camera, blew off the surface dust with an air-bulb and glanced at the Jeep.

"*Erstaundlich,*" he said, focusing the camera on the hood of the Jeep where the paint had scraped off. "Astounding." He stepped back and declared, "It has been sanded," and gave a sage nod.

But Lily was looking straight ahead at the small dune across from the Jeep. The sand had blown away from the edge of the dune, and what she saw was a sandaled foot attached to a leg buried underneath.

Chapter Two

Gideon spoke first, his voice a whisper, as if he were afraid of disturbing the dead. "A Bedouin."

"How can you tell?" Lily asked.

"His sandal, his darker skin."

"What do you suppose happened?"

"These Bedouin," Klaus said. "They're always killing each other. One tribe against another. They steal, they kill, they fight over anything—honor, revenge, a lost camel."

Gideon stared at him for a moment, then shook his head. "This is no honor killing. This is murder. Whoever did it tried to hide it by covering it."

"Murder?" Lily shivered.

A dark silhouette appeared on the horizon above the ridge of hills behind the dunes, this time on the north. A man on a camel loped toward them, his outline shimmering in the desert heat like a ghost.

Gideon gestured toward the rider. "We'll find out soon enough. Rescue is at hand."

When the man drew closer, the camel slowed, striding with the dignity of a king.

The rider wore the long khaki coat, the *jubba* of the Desert Patrol. Red bandoliers crisscrossed his chest, a dagger was inserted into his heavy red belt, a rifle was slung over his shoulder.

"Surprising," said Klaus, "that the man isn't covered with dust. These Bedouin ride out the dust storms in depressions, you know, or behind a rock until the dust devil passes." He took the scarf from around his neck, wiped at his face, and called out, "The whirlwind passed by you?"

He strode toward the Bedouin. His scarf fluttered to the ground and fell on the dune, covering the sandaled foot.

The Bedouin couched the camel and came toward them. A red-checked kafiya, folded at a slant covered his head and part of his face so that only his eyes were visible.

Gideon rose with a welcoming gesture. "*Marhaba*," he said. "Welcome in peace. *Ahlan wa Sahlan.*"

The Bedouin nodded to Gideon. "*Fik.*"

He gave no indication that he had seen the sandaled foot surfacing from the small dune near the Jeep.

"*Keif halik?* Gideon asked. "How are you?"

The Bedouin answered with a musical lilt, "*Hamdulillah.*"

"He hid in the wadi until the whirlwind passed," Klaus said into Lily's ear. "You see—I know these things."

Gideon knew the Bedouin, Jalil ibn Akram, who addressed Gideon as *tanib*, all the while facing away from the telltale dune opposite the Jeep.

Can't he see the foot, Lily wondered? She glanced at the dune again, and saw the scarf, billowing in a slight breeze, covering the bottom of the dune and the sandaled foot. Gideon gestured toward it before he spoke again.

Klaus had listened to the ritual of greeting with impatience, and now he shoved Gideon aside.

"Enough of this nonsense. Let's get going." He stood before the Bedouin, tapping his thigh. "Jalil, is it?"

Klaus told him that they were Americans doing an archaeological survey; that the axle had broken in their Jeep; that they needed transportation.

He crossed his arms and demanded to be taken to the nearest Desert Patrol Outpost, where, he said, he would arrange for a lorry to tow the Jeep and get it repaired.

Lily leaned toward Gideon, whispering, "Who does he think he is?"

Klaus sauntered to the couched camel, tied his wrapped camera to his waist, and ordered the Bedouin to take him to the Outpost. "I will facilitate arrangements from there."

He called out to Gideon, "There is only room for one of us on the camel with Jalil," and sat astride the back of the camel's saddle. "You will both be all right while I'm gone, no?"

The Bedouin looked from Gideon to Klaus and back again. "*Inshallah*," he said, and held out his hands in a hopeless gesture. "You and your sister will wait here?"

He thinks I'm Gideon's sister, Lily thought. When they had encountered their first Bedouin encampment at the beginning of the survey, Gideon reminded her that Abraham told Sarah, "Say, I pray thee, that thou art my sister." She asked him then if it was because, like Abraham, he was afraid he would be killed out of jealousy because she was so beautiful.

He had flicked an eyebrow. "Sometimes, when the sun shines golden on your hair, you have an ethereal beauty."

"Ethereal beauty?"

"And your suntan complements the sea-blue of your eyes."

"Sea-blue?"

"As blue as the Mediterranean."

Lily blushed.

"And with that color in your cheeks, you're even prettier."

He flashed a mischievous grin and ducked his head. "Satisfied?"

He held out his hands, palms up. "It's just for your own safety. Necessary if we travel together."

That time, Klaus agreed with Gideon. "A blonde might have trouble with these Arabs," he said, flapping an arm in the direction of the encampment and pontificating on the ways of the Bedouin. "Without the protection of a relative, you would appear as a woman of loose morals, fair game, taken advantage of, attacked in the night."

And now, as Jalil strolled back to the camel, mounted, and got ready to leave, Gideon shrugged. "Not much choice. *Ma'a es salaam*, Go in peace," he said to Jalil. "You'll come back for us with a lorry?"

With a mighty heave, the camel rose, lurching backward and forward as Klaus held on and grumbled.

"I hope he's as uncomfortable as he looks," Lily murmured as Jalil turned the camel north and they lumbered back up the wadi. "If he weren't a refugee from the Nazis, he could be an SS man. I almost heard the heels of his sandals click."

Gideon smiled. "He can be hard to take. But have a little understanding. In Germany, he was a Great Dane."

"A what?"

"You don't know the story? Two refugee dogs met in the park, a Saint Bernard and a little dachshund, and the dachshund looked up at the Saint Bernard and said, 'In Germany I was a Great Dane.'"

"You certainly know how to tell a story."

They watched Klaus and the Bedouin ride out of sight behind the ridge. Gideon rose, tentatively brushed some sand from the dune in front of them, to reveal part of the sandaled foot, and then opened the back of the Jeep where they stored their equipment.

Sighing, Lily followed.

He reached into the storage area, handed Lily a trowel and two brushes, and poured the last few drops from the water bags into their canteens.

They plodded back to the dune, knelt down, and began to remove the sand, moving up from the feet as if they were excavating a tomb, carefully scraping away the overburden with trowels, sweeping away the sand that lay against the body with soft paintbrushes and a rat-tailed brush.

Lily said as they kept working, "He called you *tanib*. What was that about?"

Gideon cleaned sand from the hem of the worn white *thobe*, the long Bedouin shirt that covered the body. "When I started doing surveys of Trans-Jordan a few years ago, I would go from Bedouin camp to Bedouin camp asking where to find ancient remains." He continued brushing, slower now. "They saw I needed their help. A *tanib* is someone who pitches a tent near the encampment and is under the protection of neighboring tents."

They worked silently, wielding trowels and brushes, taking an occasional sip of water. The body wore a coarse brown cloak over the *thobe*.

Lily's hand began to quiver as she realized that the clothes looked familiar. A frisson of apprehension ran through her.

"We haven't seen Qasim since he made coffee this morning," she said.

Gideon glanced at her, said nothing, and continued brushing, more carefully now.

Lily thought of Qasim's elaborate gesture as he would pour the coffee into the little porcelain cups, how he always polished the blackened coffee pot with desert sand and would tell her when he rubbed the lid that if it didn't have the figure of a chicken on the top, it wasn't a Bedouin pot.

"Qasim said he had a message for you," Lily said.

"He didn't tell me. What was it?"

She kept brushing. Slowly, carefully.

"I'm not sure, something about the Rashidi. I didn't get all of it. He spoke in a low voice, and was talking into the wind."

They had cleared the sand away from the rope that was used as a belt, and came to the hands, slightly raised, clenched in a grotesque empty grip that clutched nothing but air.

"This is beginning of rigor." Gideon paused and sat back on his heels. "When the fingers curl like that. He's been dead at least three hours." He stopped, seemed to think about it, then nodded. "In this heat, about three hours."

Lily shuddered with a flicker of dread. "Since this morning."

He glanced at Lily, his eyes dark with worry, and patted her arm in reassurance.

They cleaned the stiffened hands gently, using a camel's hair brush between the fingers, and continued along the arms and across the chest, up to the shoulders, and beyond the neck to reach the face.

They brushed away the sand to reveal a mouth distorted into the grimace-like rictus of rigor mortis. The eyes had already begun to sink. A dollop of blood at his nose had dried into a brown crust.

Lily felt the blood drain from her face. She murmured, "Qasim," and put down her brush.

Gently, Gideon cleared the sand from the open eyes as well as he could.

Lily glanced away. She could just make out a Bedouin seated on a camel watching them from the top of the ridge. His brown *kafiya* was done up as a turban and his dark cloak fluttered in the wind. She rose and stood beside of the Jeep, leaning her head against the doorpost. Even though the Jeep was hot to the touch, a chill ran through Lily and she began to tremble.

And what was the message Qasim had for Gideon, she wondered? Maybe Klaus heard some of it. I'll ask him.

Dimly, Lily heard the sound of a lorry coming down the wadi toward them and looked up.

She glanced toward the top of the ridge again. The Bedouin with the brown *kafiya* was gone. Maybe she imagined him. Gideon hadn't seen him. Who was he, and why was he watching them, she wondered?

The lorry came closer. Jalil was driving. He turned the lorry and backed it until it almost touched the front bumper of the Jeep. He reached behind him for a chain, gave a quick glance to Qasim's body with a sharp intake of breath. He looped the chain over the bumper of the Jeep and fixed it to the tow bar of the lorry before he walked over to Qasim and stood over him.

"To bury a man is to honor him," he said, and strolled to the back of the Jeep. Without a word, he signaled to Gideon and waited for him to bring out shovels and trenching spades.

He watched silently as Lily and Gideon measured out a rectangle with a north-south axis large enough for a grave and marked the area with nails and a string.

All three of them began to dig. Out of habit, Lily reached for the trowel and began to scrape the sides of the rectangle to make a plumb surface.

Jalil gave her a disapproving glance and told her to wait in the lorry.

She sat in the front seat, next to the open door, watching as the heat of the day lightened, thinking, with a touch of resentment, *he sent me away because I am a woman.*

By the time Gideon and Jalil finished digging, the sun was lower on the western horizon, and a gentle afternoon wind hinted of the cool desert night to come. Gideon cleared the string surrounding the pit and wound it around the nails, while Jalil prepared to remove Qasim's clothes to leave on top of the grave for other needy Bedouin, in Qasim's last act of generosity.

Jalil rolled the body over and spoke for the first time. "Knife wounds. More than one. He's been stabbed repeatedly in the back." He rotated it back again and left the bloodstained clothing in place.

Qasim stared with blank, sand encrusted eyes at the open sky. Both Gideon and Jalil carried him, now stiff with rigor, to his grave and lowered him into it with his head facing south toward Mecca.

Jalil wrapped the cloak tighter around Qasim before they refilled the cavity with sand heaped over the body. He piled stones over the small mound and, with his arms crossed over his chest, mumbled a prayer, first at the foot of the mound, then at its head.

Jalil turned, cleared his throat, said, "Gideon Weil, I regret that, for now, I must arrest you for the murder of Qasim ibn Achmad," and moved Gideon to the lorry.

Chapter Three

Trans-Jordan lies east of the Jordan River, east of the Dead Sea, east of the deep declivity of the Wadi Arava. Four fifths of it is desert. East of the deep valleys of the Jordan River, the Dead Sea, and the Wadi Arava, the land rises to 4000 feet, studded with villages and green with small farms, vineyards, and fig orchards cut into the terraced hillsides. Beyond that, in the rain shadow of the mountains, the hills descend almost imperceptibly into a scrub desert some twenty to twenty-five miles east of the ridge. The Hejaz railroad runs along this boundary between the desert and the sown.

This is the land of the Bedouin.

The lorry whined its way up the Wadi Rum, disturbing the elegant silence of the desert. Behind them, the Jeep wobbled against the tow-chain and stirred a cloud of dust in their wake.

For a while, none of them spoke.

As they bumped along toward the Outpost at Rum, Lily wondered how Jalil knew that the body was Qasim's. Did Klaus tell him? And what made Jalil think that Gideon had killed Qasim? Did Klaus say that too?

"Why did you arrest Gideon?" Lily asked from the back seat.

Jalil swerved to avoid a boulder in their path and the Jeep rattled behind them. "To keep the peace. An unsolved death like Qasim's could start a round of feuds among the Bedouin unless someone is held responsible."

"But why Gideon?"

"He had the opportunity."

"We didn't see Qasim all day. I was with Gideon the whole time. Why not accuse me too?"

Jalil turned his head slightly to glance at her. "You're a woman. A woman couldn't attack a man powerfully enough to kill."

Lily bristled. "Yes I could," she said, defending her right to be accused of murder, before she realized how foolish it sounded.

All this time, Gideon, his eyes wide, his mouth open in astonishment, had been staring at Jalil. "It makes no sense. Why would I kill him? I had no motive. He was our guide."

"You can argue that it was accidental."

In the distance, Jebel Rum loomed ahead of them.

"It won't be so bad," Jalil said after a while. "You'll just pay a fine to Qasim's *khamsa* for the loss of one of their members."

"But why Gideon?" Lily asked again.

"All Americans are rich." He banged on the steering wheel, sending drifts of dust into the air. "Howeitat are poor."

The rest of the way, they rode in silence.

As they came closer to Jebel Rum, the sheer red cliff of the mountain seemed to climb into the sky and beyond. Lily caught a glimpse of the Outpost of the Desert Patrol at the base, tucked up against the mountain so closely that it seemed that the mountain might fall and bury it.

From this far away, the building looked small and derelict, like the forgotten toy of a careless child.

On their right, the first signs of darkness appeared in the eastern sky.

As they drew closer, the scrub vegetation that surrounded the Outpost emitted the sharp aroma of broom and tamarisk and thorn bushes. Lily made out a squat building of large cinderblocks with turrets at the corners and a round cistern on the roof. The yard outside had a pump house, a well surrounded by mint, and a trough for watering animals. A bucket and a washbasin sat next to the well. An old, faded blue Buick was parked a short distance away. Jalil's camel was nowhere in sight.

"Where's your camel?" Lily asked.

Jalil grinned. "The desert is a haunted place. Don't you know that at night, djinn leap out of the chasms and caves to steal away with our camels?"

Gideon turned toward Jalil. "It isn't night yet. Where's Klaus?"

"He said he had business, an appointment, and rode out on the camel. Like a djinn."

"Did the djinn who rode the camel take anything with him?"

"His camera and some water."

"He say where he was going?"

"Just left. Down the wadi and over the hill."

Jalil led them inside to the back of the building and escorted Gideon to a room on the far side of an office. Lily could see the bare cinder block walls through the half-open door. The room had a high window, a sleeping palette, and two buckets near a water spigot.

Jalil escorted Gideon inside, then locked the door.

He showed Lily to the front of the building. Her room had a bed with a straw mattress, whitewashed walls, a real sink with a bucket next to it, and a drain in the center of the cement floor.

"You can wash," Jalil said. "The cistern on the roof holds a day's supply of water. Don't drink it. I keep boiled water in the kitchen for drinking." He started to leave and then turned back. "There's an outhouse behind the building. Be sure to use plenty of lime."

Jalil left, with the promise of a meal in perhaps an hour.

Lily went outside to retrieve the washbasin, brought it back to her room and filled the basin with water, still hot from the day's sun that beat on the flat roof.

She rummaged in her duffel bag for a soap dish and sponge, and laid out a towel and clean clothes on the mattress: jodhpurs, a shirt and a change of underwear.

She stepped out of the sand-heavy clothes she wore and into the basin, squeezing water from the sponge over her hair and neck, down her shoulders and back, along her legs, feeling the delightful bite of the hot water, and wondered about Klaus.

Where did he really go when he took off, the way he did today from the Outpost? He had done it before, left them for the day, and returned, with no explanation other than a shrug.

She and Gideon joked about it sometimes, speculating that he went out to meet a lady in the desert wilderness, where they made wild love all night long without ruffling his moustache.

Evenings, when they sat around the campfire, Klaus would tell them how he had escaped from Germany, how he had to leave his wife and son behind, how the Hagganah, the Jewish secret defense force, smuggled him out and landed him in Palestine on the beach at Nahariya on a moonless night. He had gone to Jaffa, he said, and gotten a job as a photographer's assistant at Balian Studios, learned Arabic by dealing with the customers, and learned Hebrew by writing down each new word he heard on a pad he always carried and looking up the word in a dictionary.

Then he would show them a picture of his wife and his son, running his fingers lovingly over their image in the flickering firelight. "They'll be all right," he would say. "They live in the country with my wife's family. They're not Jewish, you know." And then he would sigh, put the picture back in his wallet, and take it out again the next night.

Lily soaped herself and released more water from the sponge, soaped and washed again and again until the water in the basin was clouded with sand. Finally, she stepped out of the basin, dried herself, and dressed.

<>◇<>

She was surprised to find Gideon in the kitchen, helping Jalil with dinner.

Jalil lined a large platter with flat Bedouin bread piled it high with mutton, eggs, and rice and set it in the center of the table. He put a warmed, damp towel at each place.

They ate with their hands, folding a piece of the bread around the rice and mutton, their hands greasy with mutton fat, laughing as it ran down their chins with each portion, reaching for the damp towels between mouthfuls.

When they finished, Jalil brought out cups of sticky-sweet tea that left Lily thirstier for drinking it, and they leaned back and talked.

"Where does the water come from?" Lily asked. "You truck it in to the cistern every day?"

"There's a high water table here," Gideon told her, "with springs and wells. *Ain esh-Shallaleh*, the Spring of the Waterfall. It's called Lawrence's Well by some. He used Rum as headquarters for a time during the last war." He tilted his chair back precariously, then leaned forward. The chair legs landed on the floor with a bang. "There's a Nabatean temple here dedicated to the Lady Allat, and some Thamudic inscriptions."

"The Lady Allat?" asked Lily.

"The Lady Allat, the daughter of God, Goddess of the Moon, the maiden, the mother, the wise woman. She's all these things. She's even mentioned in the Koran. Herodotus called her the Arabian Aphrodite."

"You've been here before?"

Gideon nodded. "At the Nabatean Temple."

Lily thought about it, and about Gideon helping Jalil in the kitchen instead of being locked in the room on the other side of the outpost.

"You'll show me the temple tomorrow?"

"No," he said. "Tomorrow, you will go to Petra."

"Petra?"

"A wonderful place," Jalil said. "*Al-medina al-wardah*, the legendary rose-red city."

"But why?" she asked him.

"Glubb Pasha says you must learn to shoot a gun."

Chapter Four

Lily turned the key in the old Buick and pulled out the choke. It whined and coughed and finally caught.

Jalil leaned into the car and smiled. "Be careful." He gestured toward the road. "A *ghula*, a witch, dwells hidden in the caves, lying in wait, ready to jump out and devour whoever passes by." And then he laughed. "If you enter the cave of a witch you will not leave alive." He threw out his arms in a helpless gesture and laughed again. "Maybe."

After a quick breakfast of eggs and what was left of last night's bread, Jalil had told her about the car that was parked in the yard of the Outpost early this morning. It was an old Buick, he said, that belonged to Glubb Pasha.

Jalil had made a pot of Bedouin coffee, boiled up three times and laced with sugar and cardamom. He gave the first cup with the foam to Lily, making a show of pouring it from a height to create the froth.

She suspected that the offering was a bribe of some sort, that she was going to be asked to do something difficult. Gideon confirmed the suspicion when he spread out a British Ordinance Map on the table.

"Jalil has already filled the canvas bag and your canteen with water," Gideon told her. "And boiled you some extra eggs for the trip."

"What trip?"

"Abu Huniak radioed me," Jalil said. "You're borrowing his old Buick. I filled it with petrol."

"Abu Huniak?"

"Glubb Pasha. We call him Abu Huniak, little jaw. Part of his jaw was shot off in the Great War." Jalil ran his fingers along the thick stubble on the right side of his chin to demonstrate. "He doesn't mind if we call him that. We do it with love."

Glubb Pasha was Colonel John Glubb, British officer and commander of the Arab Legion, who had trained Bedouin to form the Desert Patrol.

"You're going to meet him in Petra," Gideon told her. "He's waiting for us."

"For us?" She felt less apprehensive about the trip. "You're coming with me?"

Gideon threw up his arms in a helpless gesture, raised his eyebrows in question and smiled at Jalil.

Jalil smiled back at him. "El Tanib is under arrest," he said to Lily. "You must go alone." He leaned back and sipped his coffee. "You're going to Petra! The glory of the Nabateans, the ancient masters of the desert". He leaned forward again, his face animated. "The red-rose city, half as old as time," he added, quoting a Victorian poet, much to Lily's surprise.

"Actually," Gideon said, "the first signs of occupation were in the sixth century B.C.E., probably Edomite. The Nabateans probably showed up sometime in the fourth century B.C.E."

Gideon had excavated Nabatean sites, written a book and numerous articles about them.

"Some say the Nabateans came out of Saudi Arabia, predatory camel-nomads who raided and traded frankincense and myrrh from Arabia Felix. Others say they are descendants of the Edomites. And some say they are mentioned in the Bible, as the Nebaioth, one of the sons of Ishmael."

In Roman times, the Nabateans controlled the desert trade of Imperial Rome. They built watchtowers to monitor caravans that crossed the desert tracks, stopping them for tribute. The Nabateans grew wealthy exacting payment for access to water from springs and wells, and for stops at caravanserai. They extorted tolls for perfumes brought from Arabia, for spices and silks that had traveled from India and China along the Silk Route as they crossed the desert on the way to Mediterranean ports.

Petra was the Nabatean capital.

Jalil turned back to the map. "There's a track out of here leading north. Follow it until you reach a large wadi, where the track turns left." He traced the route on the map with his finger. "Keep going."

"Here it turns north again." Gideon indicated a curve on the map. "Pass Jebel Quweira and the remains of a Roman fort. The track forks here at Ras An Naqb." He pointed to the spot. "There's a steep slope and a wadi on the right fork. Take the fork to the left." He leaned back with a wistful smile. "That's Nabatean country."

Lily wondered how she could go off to Petra without Gideon. He was the expert on the Nabateans.

"From there, it's a straight shot to Wadi Musa." Gideon looked inquiringly at Jalil. "You need this map? Can she take it with her?" When Jalil nodded, Gideon reached into a pocket for his pen, and began to ink in the route. "You'll pass two villages on the way. Here." He circled two small spots on the map with his pen. "And here."

<><><>

The drive along the hard packed desert pavement took less time than Lily had imagined. By early afternoon, she had reached Wadi Musa, the Valley of Moses, just east of Petra.

In the midst of stark desert crags, a little brook, derived from numerous springs, ran through a narrow ravine with a small village of mud-brick houses. According to tradition, this was the place where Moses smote the rock to bring forth water for parched Israelites on their way to the Promised Land after they fled Egypt. Now the copious water from the springs of Moses irrigated terraced fields planted with grapes, figs, and olives.

Lily stopped next to a large house near the entrance to the village where Gideon had told her someone would be waiting.

Behind the mud-brick wall that encircled the compound, she saw outbuildings and a courtyard with sway-backed horses buzzing with flies and tied to a hitching post.

After a few moments, an older Bedouin emerged from the house, threw horse blankets stiff with sweat on two of the horses, saddled them, attached some lengths of frayed rope as rudimentary bridles, and came smiling toward her.

He bowed with an elaborate gesture, sweeping his cloak behind him with one hand, extending the other toward her in greeting.

His long hangdog face was framed by patches of hair that were neither beard nor stubble, his dark eyes looked as if they were on the verge of tears. A faint mustache quivered above his upper lip. His face had all the discreet pathos of a basset hound.

"*Ahlen we Sahlen,*" he said. "You are most welcome." He glanced at the Buick and back at her. "Abu Huniak said you will be wanting a horse to take you through the Siq."

He went back to the horses and led out the saddled pair, Arabians who had seen better days. Their unwashed coats, sore with bare spots, had an acrid stench, their once-proud tails were sagging, and their long Arabian faces were sad and menacing.

The Bedouin cupped his hands for her to mount and gave her a boost. She landed with an ungainly bounce in the saddle. He mounted the other Arabian and reached for her makeshift bridle to lead her into the Siq, a cleft in the earth created by some long-ago earthquake.

"*Ismi Awadh el Bdoul,*" he said as they passed through the Bab es-Siq into the shade of the canyon. "*Shu ismik?* What is your name?"

Lily nodded. "*Ismi Lily.*"

They rode past the spare remains of a monumental arch hewn out of the living rock by the Nabateans that once had topped the entrance to the Siq. Around a curve, they came upon three massive carved blocks that stood in front of the facade of a rock-cut tomb, and Awadh began to sing.

"Careful when we pass here," Awadh sang. "Those blocks were carved by djinn." His nasal voice sang out as he said in a tuneless song, "No one knows what they will do. Djinn are fiery spirits, older than beasts. They are smokeless fire, like electricity. Very dangerous. They can burn your soul." He reached into a sack on his belt for some worry beads, and kept on singing. "I can take care of them. The djinn, they are afraid of song."

The horses plodded on, weary under the weight of their riders, the sound of their hoofs echoing off the cliff walls, past a tomb carved into the rock then around a bend as the Siq began to narrow.

Some votive niches were hewn into the rock. Dwarfed by the high walls of the Siq, Lily looked up. The sides leaned toward each other like an enormous corbelled arch, blocking out the light.

The remains of water channels that had brought water into Petra from the spring at Wadi Musa were cut into the sidewalls. As they clomped through the narrow winding gorge, claustrophobic within its towering walls, Lily noticed the faint deposits left from the levels of water that had run through the Siq during countless winters.

Sometimes water poured through the Siq in a roaring flash flood when a desert torrent raged. Lily recalled the story of Madame X who was drowned in the Siq during a sudden downpour. No one knew who she was, and now she was buried in one of the tombs of the Iron Age cemetery on the grounds of the École Biblique in Jerusalem next to Pere Vincente.

Would there be a flash flood today, and would she be buried there in Jerusalem, next to Madame X, as Madame Y, in The Tomb of the Unknown Tourists?

"Are there flash floods here often?" she asked Awadh.

"No, never." He kicked his horse to speed it up and gave a pull on Lily's rope. "Only sometimes."

The Siq seemed to go on forever, darker and narrower, in some places with room for only one horse at a time. Awadh handed her the rope that served as a bridle for her horse and let her lead as the horses trudged further and further. At last, around a twist in the narrow chasm, Lily saw a shaft of bright yellow sunlight.

Awadh hung back and smiled.

And then, around the next bend, at the end of the narrow cleft of the Siq, she saw it and took in her breath.

There, in front of her, rosy-bright in the afternoon sun, cut into the living rock of red sandstone was the Khazneh, the magnificent rose-pink *Khazneh el-Far'un*—the Pharaoh's treasury.

Rising to the sky, with steps leading to a columned portico, and a second story above, it looked like a Roman temple. It was a tomb fit for a king, rich and powerful, perhaps the tomb of Aretas IV Philopatris, King of the Nabateans and friend of the people.

And on the top of the Khazneh with its cornice on either side was a huge urn carved in the rock above the central *tholos*. The Bedouin thought it held the treasure of the Pharaohs.

Chapter Five

Inside the valley, Awadh dismounted. He held the rope on Lily's horse with one hand and reached for her elbow with the other in a clumsy attempt to help her alight.

"You see there?" He pointed to the urn carved into the rock of the Khazneh. "The great pharaoh of Egypt hid his treasure there."

Lily stared at the legendary Khazneh, at the urn pockmarked with rifle shots, at the Bedouin standing in front of it, dwarfed by its monumental columns, and started toward it. It was like walking in a dream.

Awadh was talking to her, but she didn't hear him.

She had seen the painting by David Roberts, who immortalized the Romantic Arab for Queen Victoria, where Bedouin in colorful clothing lolled on the steps or pointed rifles at the urn, waiting for it to break open like a piñata and shower them with gold. Now the Kazneh stood before her, elegant in its classic carvings, its floral capitals, while Awadh droned on and she ignored him.

Finally his voice roused her from her reverie. "When you finish here," he was saying, "say to anyone '*Bukrah al mishmish,*' and he will come get me."

He leaned forward, waiting for an answer.

"What does that mean, *bukrah al mishmish?*"

He tied the horses to a hitching post across from the Khazneh, hobbled them, sloshed some water into a tin watering trough.

"Does it mean anything?" she asked, and turned to look at the Kazneh once more.

"Nothing," he shrugged. "Nothing at all." His words hung in the air as he turned and started to walk up the valley.

Lily followed him for a while along the Street of the Façades that was lined with monumental rock-hewn tombs, some with false fronts like temples, some with crenellated decoration and a simple gabled door, some with engaged columns and crow-step decoration.

A strange roseate aura was reflected from the pink limestone of the surrounding rock. Lily was spellbound by the mystique of Petra. She thought of the quixotic early nineteenth-century explorers who, disguised as Arab pilgrims, rediscovered this hidden place for God and country.

Here and there, she saw footholds carved into the rock next to the tombs for climbing the cliffs or for holding scaffolding. Gideon had told her that the elaborate facades had been carved from the top down.

Up ahead, she saw Awadh near the remains of the Roman theatre where the valley curved to the right and rose to where the city began.

Someday, when she had more time, she would come back and explore the city. She would climb to the High Place, visit the temple of the god Dushara that the Bedouin called the Palace of the Pharaoh's Daughter. She would walk along the colonnaded Paved Street built for Hadrian's visit in 130 C.E. Before Hadrian, in 106 C.E., the Emperor Trajan had absorbed Nabatea into the Roman Empire, swallowed it whole like a snake ingesting its prey.

As Awadh trudged along toward the eastern bank of tombs, he passed a gang of adolescents, unwashed and scrawny, who seemed to be playing a rough sort of game. One of them had a soccer ball, which he would bounce and toss with both hands at one of the other boys.

They shouted something at Awadh as he passed. He shook his fist at them, shouted back, and continued up the valley past the theatre.

The one with the ball threw it at Awadh. It landed in the middle of his back, hard enough to knock him off balance. He didn't turn around. He staggered, squared his shoulders with an effort, and kept walking toward the elaborate set of tombs beyond the theatre. Lily watched him until he was out of sight and around the bend in the path to the city, and the adolescents disappeared into the ruins of the theatre, laughing.

As she walked along Lily pictured ancient Petra with the noise of workmen busy chiseling the great facades, cutting into the rock to hollow out interiors. She visualized the funerary processions, lines of camels stepping in somber pageant along the valley. She imagined what it would have been like then: the early Nabateans using Petra as hideaway for a nomadic Hole in the Wall Gang, and later, when the Nabateans were the proud rulers of the desert and its caravans, with Petra as their capital, a city with gardens and burbling fountains.

And here in this valley, in these rock-cut tombs that looked like temples, they buried their dead.

What were they like, these ancient Nabateans? Were they the descendants of the Edomites? Were they like the Saudis, with white kafiyas and flowing white cloaks?

She had read about them in Roman histories. It was rumored that they were cruel and avaricious, that they had captured Judeans as they fled from a burning Jerusalem and slit the captives up the belly to see if they had escaped with hidden treasure.

<>〈〉<>

A child, a girl about five years old, sat in the path in front of her. With one hand, the child scratched at a tousled mop of black curls; with the other she drew stick figures in the rosy dust. Her faded dress was streaked with the pink dust of the path. A smear of clay-colored mud smudged her cheek. She looked up at Lily with doe's eyes, smiled with tiny pearl-like teeth, stood up and smiled again.

Lily began to go around her. The child moved to the side as Lily moved to the side, back again when Lily moved back, threw out her arms and laughed. Lily took both of the child's hands and the girl tossed her head, giggling, her curls bouncing as they moved back and forth, swaying, dancing, laughing.

When Lily stopped, out of breath, she took off her hat and jammed it playfully on the child's head. The girl posed, this way and that, hands on hips.

As Lily was about to take back the hat, she remembered how the tiny disheveled girl scratched her head, and thought of head-lice. She tilted the hat on the child's head, and stood back to admire it.

"Beautiful," Lily said. "*Kawais, jameel,*" and tapped the hat to set it more carefully on the child's head.

"Keep the hat." She patted it again, and waved goodbye. "*Ma'a sa'alama.*"

The girl understood that the hat was a gift and ran off, smiling, skipping, calling "*Abou, abou,*" holding the hat in place as she ran.

Lily continued walking up the valley toward the theatre, passing the tombs hewn into the colored rock, with crow-stepped crenellations, with cornices and pediments reflecting the bright tints in the sun. In some places, she noticed the holes pecked into the rock for scaffolding for the workmen who had carved the tombs.

And crushed underfoot along the way, the ceramic remnants of the Nabatean funerary feasts, sherds of fine eggshell-thin ware, deep red, decorated with orange, or red, or dark purple-black paint depicting leaves and fronds and feathers, or tendrils and vines.

She got as far as the remains of the monumental theatre, hewn into the cliff and the face of damaged tombs. The curved tiers of the amphitheatre must have held over five thousand people.

The gang of boys that had harassed Awadh erupted out of the theatre toward her, hooting, shouting in Arabic, their leader bouncing the ball.

Lily backed up, apprehensive, then turned and rushed back down the valley where she felt safer.

She reached the Kazneh, climbed the steps to the colonnaded portico, and held onto one of the columns, panting. When she caught her breath, she checked the rooms on either side of the portico. They were empty.

Calmer, she went up more steps to the entrance to the central chamber and into the dark interior.

There was little there—open niches on each of the sidewalls to hold sarcophagi, a more elaborate one on the back wall, and an unpleasant musty smell. Nothing here to protect her.

When she came out, the gang of scruffy teenagers stood on the steps and blocked her way.

There were five of them. The one with the soccer ball bounced it once. The others fanned out in a semi-circle, cutting off any escape.

"Hello, *habibi*." The boy leered and bounced the ball again.

They moved up the steps, closing in like a pack on the hunt. The leader gave her a quick smile with rotted teeth.

She shrank into the doorway of the Kazneh.

He bounced the ball, creating a sharp retort against the rock, and moved up. She caught the stench of him—the sour breath, the fusty clothes—and she backed away into the darkness of the tomb.

Chapter Six

A rapid string of guttural Arabic, an array of curses, stopped her stalkers. The words bounced off the walls from behind them, freezing the ruffians in place.

The leader flared his nostrils, tossed his head, and flung the soccer ball at the next boy. The sharp retort of a rifle firing into the air startled him and the ball bounced down the steps into the road. Without turning, the boys stepped back and scurried after the ball, bending low to grab it.

A Bedouin holding a rifle stood in the road, his face distorted in anger. He started shooting at the dirt in front of the ball, chasing it up the valley. The boys ran after it, past the theatre, around the bend in the road, out of sight.

The Bedouin slung the rifle onto his shoulder by the strap, started up the steps toward Lily, and bowed with a flourish of his cloak and a grand sweep of his hand.

Her champion. Who is this man? "Thank you for rescuing me."

"You are our guest. I am called Adan el Bdoul." He smiled at her.

"Awadh, the man with the horses, is your father?"

"My uncle. We are all el Bdoul here. The desert belongs to the Bedouin, and Petra belongs to el Bdoul."

"Even the boys who threatened me?"

"Those boys are worthless as a cracked cup. They mean nothing." He shrugged and held out his hands, palms up. "You are

the guest of el Bdoul of Petra. No one snarls at a guest but a dog."
He dropped his hands to his sides. "You should keep your head
covered. Your hair glints golden in the sun, brings out the dogs."

She raised her hand to her head self-consciously. "You live
here?"

"I have a three cave apartment." He laughed with a proud
toss of his head. "One for a guest room, one for a bedroom, one
for a kitchen. Come, let me show you."

He led the way up the valley along the Street of the Façades
past the rock-cut tombs on the west side, past the theatre, to
the part of the valley where the tombs were arranged to the east.

"You played with my daughter," he told her. "You danced
with her and gave her a hat."

"It was nothing," Lily said.

"It made her happy."

He entered a doorway decorated with a pediment and carved
pilasters. "Come in, come in," he called to her and waved his
arm past the pilasters toward the dark interior.

It took a moment for her eyes to adjust to the dimness after
the bright glare of the valley sun. Inside was cool—the air tinged
with an odor of wet moldy stone, smoke, and spiced coffee.

A bench covered with several layers of red-striped coarsely
woven cloth ran around the inside walls. Three *loculi*, places for
ancient sarcophagi, were cut into the walls above the bench and
stacked with coarse rugs and cushions covered with cloth striped
and dyed the same deep red.

The dirt floor was swept clean. In the center was a hearth
with a blackened coffee pot beside it.

"Sit, sit," Adan said.

He took two of the cushions and placed them on the ground
near the hearth. Lily sat with her feet folded beneath her, remembering Gideon's admonition not to insult a Bedouin by showing
the bottom of her feet.

Adan lit the fire and nestled the coffee pot into it. Like Jalil,
he boiled the coffee up three times, taking it off the fire and
tapping the side of the pot each time. He poured the finished

coffee into small cups and handed Lily the first cup, the one with the most foam.

"What does *bukrah al mishmish* mean?" she asked.

Adan began to laugh. "Awadh told you that?"

"What does it mean?"

"Nothing. It's just a piece of foolishness." He took a sip of coffee. "It means nothing. It means 'tomorrow the apricots.'"

Sitting on the ground, even on cushions, felt uncomfortable, straining her legs. A physical anthropologist once told her that westerners who sit in chairs don't have squatting facets—modifications of the anklebone, like some Asians and Africans have, so they are unable to squat without strain for more than thirty seconds. Now she understood.

The coffee was hot and sweet, spiced with a lingering taste of cardamom. She sipped it, savored it, and sipped again. She put down the cup and shifted her legs to kneel on the pillow with her feet behind her.

"The *tanib* is not with you?" Adan asked.

"He stayed behind in Rum."

Adan poured a second cup of coffee, and Lily drank it slowly and carefully, adjusting her legs again.

"Someone is waiting for you here." Adan poured a third cup, this time without sugar, and Lily realized that that was a signal to leave.

"Abu Huniak. Glubb Pasha. He is waiting for you."

"Where?"

He doused the fire with what was left of the coffee and went outside. Lily followed.

They strolled down toward the Urn tomb. Two stories of arches made it look like a giant columbarium.

A man wearing a seersucker suit with a white linen vest stood in the middle of the street watching Lily. Straw-colored hair was plastered on his forehead, except for the tufts that stood straight up in a cowlick on the back of his head. It made him look like a fractious child. As Lily passed, he didn't move, but his eyes followed her. She felt his intense gaze penetrate her wake and she rubbed the back of her neck.

Adan pointed to a ledge above the arches of the Urn Tomb. "Up there."

A man was seated in a camp chair in the shade by the open flap of an olive green army tent. He wore a British army uniform topped with a red-checkered kafiya instead of a military cap. He had a thin military moustache, a slightly lop-sided jaw, and he was reading a book.

Lily turned to Adan and said, "*Bukrah al mishmish.*"

Chapter Seven

In the hotel, Lily opened a musty closet, shook her dress out of the duffle, put it on one of the wire hangers, and brought it into the bathroom to steam out the wrinkles while she showered and bathed. She intended to do both.

Colonel Glubb had driven her to the hotel in Amman in his old Buick to arrange for her to speak to His Majesty, Emir Abdullah, about Gideon being held at Rum.

The dress, pale green, had cost five dollars—the sort of dress her mother would have called unacceptable and gauche. But it had sleeves that covered her elbows, a high mandarin collar, and reached down to her mid-calf, modest enough for an Arab city like Amman. The belt was a sort of sash that wound around her waist twice and tied in a loop.

Tomorrow, she would go to a palace and talk to a king. She should have gone to the souk and bought something else. Too late for that.

The bathroom was a step up from the bedroom, to accommodate plumbing under the floor, she supposed. The soap had a drawing of olives on the wrapper and smelled of jasmine. In the shower, she worked up a lather with the flimsy washcloth, savoring the perfume, rubbing the cloth against her skin, worrying about Gideon, wondering what she could say to the Emir to have him released.

Iridescent bubbles formed and burst and washed in a stream to a drain in the middle of the floor. She watched the water swirl counter clockwise down the drain, remembering Rafi. He would stand at the kitchen sink finishing the dishes, swishing the water counterclockwise, trying to make it turn against nature. Numb with grief, she still expected to find him everywhere: across a fruit stand at a souk, sitting in a chair in the next room, his hands resting on the wooden arms. But he was gone, vanished in the furious hellhole of el Alamein, never to return.

She dried with the thin hotel towel and crept into bed. Three box-like sections of ticking filled with straw crackled when she moved, and the tired springs creaked and groaned with each shift of her body. She slept fitfully, waiting for morning, dreaming of Rafi again, dreaming that he was still alive, that el Alamein had never happened, that there was no war, that they were still in Jerusalem.

In the morning, she clambered into the ball-and-claw tub, holding on to the high rim with both hands. The water was luke-warm and rusty and when she got out, she slipped on the tile floor, reached out and caught herself on the edge of the sink. Was this how the day would go? Stumbling, righting yourself just in time?

She put on the pale green dress, dumped the dirty clothes from the duffel on the bed to be laundered, and went downstairs. Breakfast in the garden there included strong coffee, pickled fish, and cheese, with fresh butter on a crisp, circular roll covered with sesame seeds.

Colonel Glubb came for her at ten in a gleaming black Packard town car, with tiny Trans-Jordan flags fluttering atop the front fenders.

At the palace, a guard from the Desert Patrol saluted, opened the door ceremoniously and motioned them through. Glubb led her down a long corridor, moving briskly past wall hangings of silk rugs woven into garden scenes or portraits of the royal family, past arched windows that framed a bright rose garden. Breathless, Lily scurried to keep up.

"There's nothing to be afraid of." Glubb turned and gave her a reassuring smile. "He's a gentleman all through. When he first came to Trans-Jordan, he held court Bedouin style on the outskirts of Amman."

Glubb slowed. Lily caught up with him and they walked in step. She realized that they were marching.

"Trans-Jordan has changed since Abdullah took over. Things are orderly now. He's a good ruler. When he came here, there were four rivals factions. He achieved a measure of unity. Different from the infighting of other Arab countries."

They had reached the end of the corridor where a guard stood before an ornate pair of carved wooden doors.

"Wait here," Glubb said. The guard stood aside. "I'll see if His Majesty is ready."

Glubb disappeared into the room beyond, and the guard resumed his position before the doors and in front of Lily. His legs apart, his rifle cradled at a slant, he stood motionless, staring at Lily. A bee buzzed along the corridor and danced between them. From the garden, Lily thought.

The guard's eyes followed the bee and he smiled at Lily. When it landed on his shoulder, he flicked it off with snap of his finger and winked at Lily. She stepped back.

The guard opened the double doors. With a sweep of his arm, he invited Lily to enter the room beyond—a long room with a travertine floor. Tables with mother of pearl inlay, armchairs with tasseled cushions, and elaborate folding chairs were scattered on a pair of fine, palace-size Nain silk rugs. Along one long wall, windows with graceful pointed arches bordered with mosaics opened onto a dappled garden with a pool and fountains. A large inlaid ebony desk surrounded by tiles set into the wall stood against another.

At the far end of the room, the Emir was seated on a dais in a cushioned chair with mother-of-pearl inlays. A handsome child with dark, liquid eyes—his grandson, Prince Hussein—clung to the leg of his chair and rested his head on the Emir's knee. The Emir's son, Crown Prince Talal, sat cross-legged on a cushion on his right, and Glubb Pasha moved to stand behind him on his left.

Lily was offered a seat below the dais to the right of the Emir.

The Emir leaned forward. "And how is my friend Gideon Weil?" His smile encouraged Lily.

"He's been arrested."

The Emir frowned. "How? Where? What happened?"

"Our guide was killed and a man from the Arab Legion arrested Gideon. They're holding him at the fortress at Rum."

"Your guide was a Howeitat. They are the traditional enemies of the Beni Sakhr," the Emir said, as if that explained everything. "I shall send word to the guard at Rum, tell him to release my friend."

He stroked the tumble of curls on his grandson's head and leaned back. A soft smile played on his lips when Hussein looked up at him. "Once we were more powerful than the British," he said to the child in a soft voice. "We have a long and proud history."

He sighed, stood up, strolled to the window and gazed at the play of water in the fountain. "We have everyone here. Moslems, Christians, Armenian artisans, Druze from the mountains, Circassian warriors, gentlemanly Bahai, fellahin in the towns and villages, merchants in the cities." He spoke to Lily now. "And Bedouin. We are all Bedouin. The others come and go, Romans, Crusaders, Mamelukes, Turks, Palestinians, British." He turned around to face her. "But we will be here forever."

He returned to the dais. "And we own the land." He seated himself again in the ebony chair. "The land belongs to the Bedouin."

He leaned back against the cushion and said to Lily, "I will assign a guide to you from the Beni Sakhr who is fit for the task ahead of you."

"And what is the task ahead?" Lily asked.

"Someone who knows Rum, who knows the routes, who knows the eastern desert."

So we're going to the eastern desert, that much she could gather. Secrets, secrets, she was surrounded by secrets. Well, there's a war on. What did that poster say? A slip of the lip can sink a ship? There were no slips, no ships here in Amman. A cat can look at a king, but it can't make him purr, she thought. Abdullah knows more about the survey for the OSS than I do.

With a wave of his hand, a smile, and a slight bow of his head, the Emir dismissed her. "*Mashallah*," he said. "May Allah preserve you. *Ma'a es salaam*. Go in safety."

Colonel Glubb accompanied her on her way out along the long corridor.

"The Hashemites are a Bedouin tribe?" Lily asked him.

"The most prestigious of them all. Far more important than the Saudis. The Saudis stole Mecca from the Hashemites. Mecca is the birthright of the Hashemites. Abdullah's father was ruler of Mecca, King of Hejaz." He stopped walking and turned to Lily. "The Prophet himself was a Hashemite, did you know that?"

She noticed that the colonel referred to Mohammed as the Prophet and thought he's been living among Moslems for a long time.

"You don't think much of the Saudis, do you?" she asked.

"They're satiated with plunder. Drunk on greed and religion."

"That's pretty harsh."

"They base their power on Wahhabism. Recent sect, eighteenth century. Ultra conservative, militaristic. As far as I can see, it's a distortion of Islam, will set them back a thousand years."

"But the British support the Saudis."

"For the oil. It seems we're running short of coals in Newcastle."

They continued down the corridor and Glubb turned to her again.

"When you get to the eastern desert," he said, "watch out for Gerta Kuntze. She's a troublemaker. She lives among the Rashidi, the Bedu on the Iraqi border, moving from tent to tent, stirring up problems. We don't need her. We have enough worries."

So, we *are* going to the eastern desert.

Glubb looked out the window for a moment, where petals from overblown roses caught in the breeze and wafted to the ground. "Kuntze thinks of herself as the modern-day Gertrude Bell. Calls herself the Empress of Mesopotamia. But she's no Gertrude Bell. For one thing, Kuntze is German, not British."

"Gertrude Bell, the woman who was called the Queen of Iraq? Lawrence's friend?"

"The very same. I met Gertrude Bell once in Cairo. She was a silly egomaniacal windbag, a virago, and the world's greatest expert."

"Expert on what?"

"Everything. Ask her anything, she knew more about it than God."

Behind them, a door closed and they heard the tap of small scampering feet.

A child's voice called out, "Wait for me, wait for me," and they turned to see Prince Hussein running toward them.

Hussein clasped Glubb's hand. "Grandfather says that Abu Hun...Glubb Pasha is a great hero," he said to Lily. "Grandfather says that he saved my cousin Faisal's life and rescued Iraq from the Germans. My cousin is the king of Iraq."

He was talking about the eight-year-old king, the grandson of Lawrence's Faisal.

"You were going to call Colonel Glubb '*Abu Huniak*,' weren't you?" Lily asked the young prince.

"It's not polite to call someone a name. Someday, I will be king, like my cousin Faisal, and kings are always polite."

"Your grandfather told you that?" Lily asked.

"Grandfather is wise and kind. He is always polite."

"Who taught you English?" Lily said. "You speak it very well."

"When the war is over, grandfather says, when it is safe in England, I will go to school there, to Harrow with my cousin Faisal. And then I shall go to Sandhurst, like Glubb Pasha, and become a great warrior."

A door along the corridor opened, and a uniformed guard approached. "Your Highness, His Majesty is looking for you."

Hussein released Glubb's hand. He went with the guard, turned back, and waved at them. "*Ma'a es salaam*," he called as Lily and Glubb watched him continue down the corridor.

Glubb waited until he was out of sight before he said, "Back to Gerta Kuntze. She stirs up the Bedu to plot against the Allies for her friend Rashid Ali al-Gaylani."

"The former prime minister of Iraq?"

"The very same, the engineer of last year's insurrection, a plot to kill young Faisal. We intervened, rescued Faisal, and sent Rashid Ali into exile."

"Rashid Ali is a Nazi sympathizer?"

"More than that. Sold Iraqi oil to the Kraut, sent Iraqi artillery against our base in Habbaniya. We took care of him last year," he said again, and laughed. "They call it the Anglo-Iraqi War. Imagine that."

She had heard about the war. Glubb led the invasion.

He stood against the window. The bright sun behind him outlined his silhouette and made it difficult for her to see the expression on his face. "Rashid Ali fled to Berlin. Now he and his friend, the Grand Mufti of Jerusalem, Haj Amin al Husseini, have tea and cakes with Hitler."

Behind Glubb in the garden blowsy Damask roses nodded in a slight breeze that blew the spray from a fountain in the center toward the ring of dark pink flowers.

"While they talk about their plans to rule the Arab world and eliminate the Jews?"

"Just so." He took a deep breath, shook his head. "None of it is easy. Lawrence had it right. We've been led into a trap in Mesopotamia that we can't escape with dignity and honor. And all the while, Gerta Kuntze travels from tent to tent, lives like a Bedu, lice and all, calling herself the Empress of Mesopotamia."

"She's an archaeologist?"

"Vocational." Glubb sighed. "Rashid Ali may be in Berlin, but he still pulls the strings in Iraq."

Lily remembered a picture she had seen of little Hussein and the young king, Faisal, standing together, arms over each other's shoulders. They looked like twins, but Hussein's eyes were laughing while Faisal's were sad and full of foreboding.

"The Arabs believe in fate. If Faisal is fated to be killed by Rashid Ali, then he will be."

"Even if it takes forty years?"

"Or less," Glubb said.

◇〉◇〉

Lily rode back to the hotel in the Packard. She sat straight in the plush beige back seat, feeling grand and a little royal, wondering if she should give a queenly bow and wave to the fellahin who gazed after them when the town car passed.

Before she went upstairs, Lily sat outside at the café across from the hotel, watching the traffic along the dusty street: old carts and new cars; men wearing three piece suites and carrying briefcases bustling along; Bedouin on sleek Arabian horses; women in Paris dresses; women wearing head scarves and embroidered abayas. And everyone walked down the center of the road, casually blocking traffic.

Amman was still a town that was building. Some streets were paved, some not yet finished; everywhere, half-built stone houses, some Turkish style, some modern Bauhaus with curved balconies and glass brick partitions.

She had ordered a crème caramel and a bottle of Jordan Valley water. While she waited, the man with the straw-colored hair who had been watching her at Petra snaked through the tables toward her.

He sat across from her and asked in faintly accented English, "Do you mind if I join you?"

There were plenty of other tables. The café was less than half filled, mostly with men, some by themselves engrossed in the newspaper; some with friends, leaning forward, speaking with eager faces and elaborate gestures.

"I'd like to talk with you," the man said.

A shepherd moved his flock slowly down the center of the thoroughfare, ignoring angry drivers blasting horns of automobiles.

The waiter brought the bottled water and crème caramel and set them in front of Lily. She fingered the cool bottle where small drops of water ran down the outside.

"About what?"

"We have much to discuss," the man with the straw-colored hair said. He leaned forward, and grabbed her hand.

She snatched it away and rubbed it on the side of her dress.

"I know who you are," he said. "You are not his sister."

He's talking about Gideon. Who was this man? What did he want?

The man looked around at the other tables, lowered his voice. "It could be to your advantage," he said. "And not too much trouble."

She felt a vague uneasiness, felt the menace underneath his soft voice.

He wants to pay me to do something underhanded? Lily didn't answer. She threw a handful of piastres on the table, grabbed the bottle of water, and stood up.

"Don't go yet," he said, reaching for her arm again.

She pulled away, ran across the street back to the hotel, her heart pumping, and left the crème caramel on the table, untouched.

◇◇◇

When she returned to her hotel room, the laundry sat on the freshly made bed, starched and ironed, and all colored a vivid electric yellow, with the orange scarf, the one that she had used to cover her face in the whirlwind, neatly folded on top. The laundress had boiled everything together.

And the next morning, in a new Jeep, a new hat tied under her chin with shoelaces she had fastened above the brim, and dazzling yellow jodhpurs and shirt bright as the morning sun, she drove back to Rum.

Chapter Eight

Lily, Gideon, and their new guide, Hamud bin Abdul Aziz from the Beni Sakhr, sat in the shade of the wall of an ancient ruin about forty kilometers north of Petra, eating a lunch of tomatoes and cucumbers and hard-boiled eggs. Klaus was lying in the sun half-propped up on one elbow, his eyes on Hamud, his face tilted up toward the sun.

"Mad dogs and Englishmen," Lily told him.

"Englishmen can't always be wrong," Klaus said. "The sun is good for the soul."

"We'll go along the King's Highway," Gideon had said when they left Rum. "Any spot of strategic value has ancient fortifications—Roman, Crusader, Turkish."

"Is that why we're here?" Lily asked. "To find locations of strategic value?"

Gideon stared at her. Is it possible that he doesn't know why we're here any more than I do, she wondered?

"Donovan picked us to work in Trans-Jordan. Because we're archeologists?" she asked.

Gideon still didn't answer.

Of course he knows why we're here. He visited Abdullah and Glubb in Amman, and left me to map the Roman theatre. He knows.

"Archaeologists can go anywhere without raising suspicion," Gideon finally said, but that was no answer.

The King's Highway led from Syria to Aqabah, from Edom to Arabia Petra, following the ridge east of the Dead Sea and the Arava along a line of freshwater springs. The Romans built Trajan's road along this route.

"Armies have come through here from the days of Moses," Gideon had remarked. "As Moses said to Sihon, king of the Amorites, 'We will go by the King's Highway until we have passed thy border.'"

Klaus rolled his eyes again. "He didn't simply let them pass, did he?"

"No, they had to fight. Israel smote the Amorites with the edge of the sword, and took their cities."

Stopping at an abandoned caravanserai, they had walked among the tumbledown walls of rooms heavy with the odor of urine, of human and animal waste piled in the corners. They sheltered against the wind near an outside wall higher than the others, and spread out their sleeping bags.

When they were putting up a tarp for protection from the ruthless desert sun, Gideon discovered that two of the tent pegs were missing. He found a fig tree planted at the derelict cistern, and broke off some branches.

"Does anyone have a knife?" he asked.

No one did. Gideon picked up a flint cobble and smashed it smartly against a boulder to get a shatter of sharp flint flakes. While Lily and Klaus watched, he used the flakes to scrape the branches smooth and whittle rough points at one end. Using another cobble, he drove the points into the ground, substituting the trimmed branches for the missing tent pegs.

Lily thought of Jael, who drove a tent peg through the head of the cruel Sisera. But this time Gideon omitted the Biblical reference, and rocked back to admire his handiwork.

"When I was a child," he said, "I wanted to be an archaeologist so that if I were lost on a desert island, I would know what to do." He tightened the rope around the peg. "And now, you see, I know what to do."

"This is not an island," Klaus said. "Just a desert."

<>‹›‹>

Gideon ran his fingers along the ashlar masonry with its polished edges and diagonally tooled bossing. "Nabatean masonry.
Reused to build this caravanserai." He turned to Klaus. "You
took a picture of this?"

"He's seeing Nabateans again," Klaus muttered. "If it isn't
Abraham or Moses, it's the Nabateans."

Klaus pointed his camera at the block of limestone, glanced
at his watch, then toward the rolling hills to the east.

"They passed through here." Gideon leaned his back against
the wall, dreaming. "They brought frankincense and spices
from Arabia to the sea or to Damascus. Early Christian pilgrims
came through here and died by the side of the road. Crusaders
fought here."

He closed his eyes, while Klaus again looked at his watch.
Gideon's voice became pensive, lost in the past. "In the old days,
before the railroad, pilgrim's caravans on their way to Mecca
would travel down this route, stopping each night at a fortified
caravanserai like this.

"They would fetch a fresh supply of water from the cistern,
water their animals, spend the night." Gideon shook himself
and stood up. "Just like us."

Klaus turned back the cuff of his shirt and glanced at his
watch yet again.

"You have a dentist appointment?" asked Lily.

Klaus gave her a puzzled look.

"You keep looking at your watch."

"It's a Schafhausen. I bought it there, you know, in
Switzerland, in Schafhausen." He looked at the east again, across
the rutted track to the flint-strewn desert. A slight breeze lifted
his hair and he pushed it back. "I escaped Germany through
Switzerland, got down the Rhine as far as Schafhausen. Boats
unload there because of the Reinfalls. It's the largest waterfall in
Europe." He paused again, his eyes focused on a distant vision.
"The Reinfalls was astonishing. The noise of the roiling water

blocked out everything. I stood on the hill of Schloss Laufen and watched the power of crashing water, flying spray boiling and churning. Draining away like my life. I wept. I never expected to, but I wept."

He moved his cuff back with his forefinger and ran it gently across the watch. "Some day, when all this is past, when the war is over, I'll sell the watch and use the money to go back home, open a camera shop and studio. This is my fortune, all that I own. It's worth a lot of money."

"You have the Exakta," Lily said, pointing to his camera.

"I bought it cheap in Jaffa from a refugee who brought it with him from Germany. He needed the money. A lot of bargains are to be had from people who brought things in."

"Like your Schafhausen?"

"That's different."

How is it different, she wondered? Could he get enough for the watch to open a camera shop?

"What was your profession before you left Germany?"

"I... I owned a department store. Two of them. I know how to run a business."

In Germany, Lily thought, Klaus was a Great Dane.

She remembered that Klaus stood behind Qasim when he was relaying the message for Gideon. "Before he died, Qasim said he had a message for Gideon. Something about the Rashidi. Do you know what it was?"

Klaus shrugged and shook his head. "How should I know? Ask Gideon."

After lunch, Klaus disappeared again.

"I know where he goes," Hamud said and winked, then began to laugh. "He goes to visit a woman."

Lily and Gideon exchanged glances and smiled. "I told you so," she said.

"He visits a Bedouin?" Lily asked.

"No, no. She calls herself the Empress of Mesopotamia. She thinks she is like al Khatan, the woman you call Gertrude Bell. But al Khatan moved among the Bedouin by bribing them with great gifts. This woman has no such wealth. She is ugly, even uglier than al Khatan, with hair the color of terra cotta and speckles all over her face and arms, as if flies had lain with her. But worst are her eyes—like cold green stone."

"What's a khatan?" Lily asked.

"A lady of the court," Gideon told her. "Gertrude Bell meddled in everything. They called her the Queen of Iraq. She was formidable, overwhelming, power mad."

"You and Glubb don't seem to approve of her."

"Iraq's troubles started with Gertrude Bell. All of today's troubles in the Middle East. At the end of the last war, she drew the borders, she decided who ruled where."

While Hamud cleaned up from lunch, Lily and Gideon explored the area beyond the caravanserai. They walked into an enclosure with the remnants of a wall.

Behind it were the remains of a square building, the walls scarred by Bedouin campfires, the corners reeking of human and animal detritus.

"A temple of the goddess Allat, consort of Dushara, the chief Nabatean god." Gideon told her. "In this courtyard they held public festivities. You see here," he pointed to the stubs of engaged columns along two of the sides. "There was a gallery above."

In the rubble of the square building, they found the vestiges of an inner shrine, surrounded by broken pieces of statuary and reliefs scattered on the ground.

Gideon pointed to the ruins of a tower behind the shrine and a stairway. "This led to the roof. In the twilight after the sun set, the priest would climb up there to make the goddess suddenly appear before the worshippers at a doorway above the temple in a sudden burst of illumination, an epiphany, lit only by fire. Then excitement and wonder would sweep through the congregation."

He spoke in a magical whisper, recreating the ecstasy of the moment in a way that made Lily's skin prickle.

"You've been reading Durkheim," she said, and he smiled. "Did they burn frankincense on the altar? Did they sacrifice a goat or a sheep?"

Gideon threw up his hands.

"Did the ceremony take place on the night of the full moon," she asked, "or during the dark of the moon?"

"Burned frankincense, maybe. It was their monopoly. Controlled the caravan routes from Arabia, that and the silk trade from China, bound for ports on the Mediterranean." He continued walking around the building, his hands in his pockets. "They dug wells and guarded them, set up serai, demanding payment from everyone who came through."

"The Saudis of the Roman world?"

"More than that. The Saudis have nothing except oil. They have no water. They have nothing but sand and rocks and oil."

"What will they do when the oil runs out?" Lily asked. "Go back to raiding, to stealing camels from the Howeitat?"

"The Nabateans were different. They were in the desert, too. After the Romans learned the secret of the monsoons and went by sea and the Nabatean monopoly was over, they farmed the desert. Built check dams and cisterns to catch the desert rain, terraces to hold the soil, planted crops."

"So, maybe fifty or a hundred years from now camel caravans will pass through here from Saudi Arabia," Lily said.

"Carrying what? Frankincense? On a route that leads nowhere? Besides, in the Arabian Peninsula there is little rain to catch in cisterns and check dams. Rainfall is less than a quarter of an inch a year."

When they got back to the caravanserai, Klaus was waiting for them, rummaging through his things, putting away his camera and a small matchbox. Gideon sent him back to take pictures of the enclosure and the temple.

"Got some interesting pictures of the terrain," Klaus said with some satisfaction, and Lily wondered about where he got the matchbox.

Chapter Nine

Lily heard a car whine its way toward the caravanserai, and turned to see Jalil emerge from Glubb's old Buick.

He carried a rifle and handed it to Lily. "This is for you."

Her arm dropped under its heft.

"A twenty-two millimeter Lee-Enfield training rifle," Jalil told her. "Number two, MK four. It's a single shot affair, only to teach you how to shoot."

She grasped the firearm with both hands, then cradled it in her arms.

"And to teach you safety and marksmanship." Gently, Jalil moved the barrel down. "First, you'll learn to shoot, later to clean, strip and load. Then maybe, you'll be issued one." He pushed the rifle down further, and pointed the barrel at the ground. "Maybe."

He unfolded a large paper target and scanned the walls of the caravanserai.

"Not there," Gideon told him. "Your ancestors built these walls. Have you no respect for your past?"

"If not there, where?" Jalil wedged the top of the target into a crack between ashlars. "Not my ancestors. The Bdoul's ancestors maybe, but not mine."

He led Lily to a place next to a boulder, about fifty yards from the target. "Stand here."

He reached for the rifle. "This is the sight," he said, pointing. "This is the trigger. It has a safety catch. Push it forward when I tell you."

He handed the gun back to her. "The rifle has a short butt. Bring it up to your right shoulder." He waited while she rested it on her shoulder, feeling the weight of it. "Your right eye should be over the heel of the butt. You should be able to see the target through the sight. Can you?"

She nodded, lost sight of the target for a second, then found it again.

"Put the first joint of your finger around the lower part of the trigger. Squeeze the trigger until you hear a distinct click."

She pulled back the trigger, heard a distinct click, and jerked in surprise.

"Lower your cheek to the butt of the rifle so that you see through the sight."

The wood of the butt was warm against her cheek.

"Keep your eye back. The discharge has a kick."

"Will I knock out my eye? After this, will I go around looking like a pirate, with an eye patch and a cursing parrot on my shoulder?"

"Too close to your face," he said. "Back it up a bit." He reached over to move the butt of the rifle back. "Close your left eye." He waited. "Aim."

She squinted through the sight.

"You see the target? Is it clearly in the center of the sight?"

She would have nodded, but was afraid that she would loose sight of the target.

"Hold your breath and continue squeezing with your right hand. Where are the sights pointing now? High? Low?"

Lily had no idea what he meant.

"Hold it firmly on your shoulder with your left hand. Keep your head still. Hold your breath."

"Suppose I begin to shake? Or run out of air?"

"Fire."

The kick knocked her back, exploded in her ear. The gun clattered to the ground.

She swallowed, took a deep breath, and sneezed. The air around her smelled like a firecracker gone wrong.

"Didn't hit the target," Gideon tried to tell her. She had trouble hearing him. "It sailed over the wall, hit something inside the caravanserai."

An echo rebounded off the canyon walls and rolled through the silence of the desert.

"Now you know the feel of it," Jalil said. "Catch your breath. I'll show you how to reload. Next time, aim down."

"I think you hit the temple," Gideon told her. "Wounded the goddess Allat, consort of Dushara."

"I'll try again," she said. "Maybe next time I'll kill her."

She saw the Bedouin before she heard him, galloping toward them on a camel, grim-faced, brandishing a rifle, the strap flapping as he bore down on them. Even the cloak flying behind him seemed angry.

The Bedouin twisted the camel's head when he pulled back on the reins, couched the camel with a gruff shout and a pull, and tripped over its front leg when he dismounted. He grabbed the strap of his rifle, flung it across his back, steadied himself, rushed at Gideon, and thrust a livid face at him.

"I am Khalid ibn Achmad, the brother of Qasim."

Lily saw the Bedouin reach over his shoulder, ready to grab his rifle to threaten Gideon.

She picked up the twenty-two at her feet, slung it into position just as Jalil had coached her, and pointed the empty gun at the Bedouin.

She closed one eye and put the other to the thingamajig used for aiming the way Jalil had told her, aimed, put her finger on the trigger, and said, "What is it you want?"

Chapter Ten

The Bedouin turned around to face Lily and narrowed his eyes. "I demand amends," he said, with a lecherous grin toward Lily, flashing tobacco-stained teeth.

"What amends?"

"For the death of Qasim. I am Khaled ibn Achmad, brother of Qasim." He looked at Gideon. "The murderer must pay."

"I, too, mourn Qasim," Gideon told him. "I had nothing to do with his death."

"You lie." Ibn Achmad spit on the ground next to Gideon's foot. "You must pay."

"Pay what?" Lily asked.

Ibn Achmad leered at Lily again. "Fifty camels and *ghurra*."

"No *ghurra*," Jalil said.

"What's *ghurra*?" Lily asked

"A girl from the family of a murderer," Jalil said. "She must marry the nearest relative of the dead man to produce a male child."

Ibn Achmad kept his eyes on Lily. "Our mother weeps for Qasim. Nothing will do this time but *ghurra*. The sister of el Tanib."

Ibn Achmad leaned in toward Gideon. "The sister of el Tanib for my brother Qasim." He thrust his thin, high nose, sharp as a weapon, in Gideon's face.

Gideon backed away. "I did not kill Qasim."

Jalil slapped his hand against his thigh impatiently. "We shall investigate Qasim's death. When we find the killer, the killer will pay fifty camels and then five more instead of *ghurra*."

Ibn Achmad threw up his arms and shook a fist. "El Tanib lies. He killed my brother."

Gideon took another step back. "I did not kill Qasim," he repeated.

"I will prove it," Ibn Achmad said. "We will do *bisha'a.*"

"What does he mean?" Lily asked Jalil.

"He wants a Howeitat trial."

"First we need three from the nose of nine." Ibn Achmad ticked off on his fingers. "Three flying, three galloping, three dismounting."

"They select three judges from a panel of nine," Jalil explained. "And then what?"

"Then we do *bisha'a,*" ibn Achmad said.

"Exactly what is *bisha'a?*"

"A way to the true light of Allah," ibn Achmad answered.

Chapter Eleven

They reached the camp of Khalid ibn Achmed near Qusayr Amra by late morning. He had arranged for a large encampment of Bedouin to gather there to bear witness to the *bisha'a*.

Qusayr Amra was the abandoned hunting lodge of the desultory eighth century Umayyad Caliph al-Walid. Lily and Gideon had been there once before during the survey, and been awed by frescoes on the domed ceilings in the bath, with paintings of animals, of naked dancing ladies, of plump, scantily clad singers clutching ouds. Klaus had busied himself with his tripod and light meter while Gideon commented that the slaves who stoked the hypercaust must have used pasturage for miles around for fuel while goats and sheep of the Bedouin starved. That day, Klaus took two rolls of film, and used all his flash bulbs, saying "ooh" and "aah" each time the flash went off, while Gideon parodied the excesses of the long dead caliph, shouting, "More heat, more heat," with an imperious gesture to slaves he pictured laboring to produce it.

◇◇◇

The encampment was located on high ground near a wadi. As they approached the camp, sounds carried on the wind: the bray of donkeys; the tired honking of camels complaining about their fortune; the bleating of sheep and goats; the clucking and crowing of wandering chickens; the call of crows, flapping and cawing and picking on garbage at the edge of the camp.

Closer to the camp, dogs chased them, barking and growling, playing tag with the wheels of the vehicles. Jalil parked the Buick down-slope, near the edge of the camp; Gideon pulled the Jeep up next to it.

"What is *bisha'a*," Lily asked Jalil as they trudged up the hill toward the camp.

"It's a fire test, a test of guilt or innocence. A red-hot piece of metal is placed against the tongue of the accused. If his tongue burns, he is guilty."

Lily shook her head, astonished. "That's trial by ordeal," she murmured. "It's medieval."

"Not to worry," Jalil said. "Gideon will come through it."

"How do you know?"

"It works on a principle similar to a lie detector. If he's lying, his mouth will be dry, and his tongue will burn. Otherwise, not."

Lily threw up her hands. "And what happens if his tongue burns?"

Jalil shrugged. "Then he's guilty. It's up to the judges. And Khalid. This has all the authority of a court procedure."

Lily heard a sharp intake of breath from Gideon.

"Have you witnessed *bisha'a* before?" she asked Jalil.

"Just a couple of times. Once, the accused burnt his tongue so badly he got blood poisoning." He thought a minute. "Actually, gangrene."

To die slowly, of hideous, evil-smelling sores. Lily glanced over at Gideon, at his pale face, at his labored breathing as he plodded up the hill, and knew that his mouth was dry with fear.

Guilty or innocent, Khalid isn't out for money or camels. He's out for vengeance.

Lily backtracked to the wadi, picking at the scrub vegetation, searching the surface of the wadi.

"What are you doing down there?" Gideon called.

She picked up a few water-washed stones. "Nothing really."

She plucked two tiny wildflowers, climbed back up, called to Gideon, "Look what I found."

She handed him the wildflowers, pressed the pebbles into his palm surreptitiously, and whispered, "Put these in your mouth. Hide them in your cheek."

He looked puzzled.

"It's an old Indian trick," she said. "I learned it from the Cahuilla Indians around Palm Springs when I was growing up. They would suck on stones when they walked in the desert to keep their mouths from going dry."

"This works?"

"Worked for them. It'll work for you."

In the camp, men were seated around campfires, blackened coffee pots ever present, talking, smoking, while women hammered tent posts, ground flour, pulled ropes hand over hand to haul buckets of water from an ancient cistern.

Black goat-hair tents clustered around a sheik's larger tent sheltered by pistachio trees on the edge of the wadi. One side of the sheik's tent was open to the breeze.

Some of the Bedouin women, green and blue tattoos around their mouths and eyes, approached Lily with laban and eggs to sell. She shook her head, clicked her tongue, repeating, "No, no. *Laa, Laa,*" then changed her mind.

"*Laban,*" she said, pointing at the bowl of soured Bedouin milk, and found a piastre in her pocket. She gave it to one of the women who handed her a dollop of laban in a soiled paper cup while chickens strutted and worried around her, pecking at the dirt.

People wearing black robes were coming and going from a tent on the edge of the encampment.

"That's the mourner's tent," Jalil said. "In the mourner's tent, they wear black. They serve only black, unsweetened coffee." He gazed at the crying women, raising their arms in despair gathered around the entrance to the tent.

"Black is the color of mourning, and death is bitter," Jalil told her, while she wondered how she could give the *laban* to Gideon without being noticed.

Gideon was still pale, still frightened. She picked up a handful of dirt, threw it toward the wadi just beyond the chickens and they scurried noisily after it, squawking, cackling, wings flapping. While the Bedouin women ran after them, she slipped the cup of *laban* to Gideon.

"What am I supposed to do with this," he asked.

"Put it in your mouth of course."

Gideon began to laugh. "When you're through with me, I'll have so much saliva, I'll dribble."

It was a nervous laugh. He'll get through it, Lily thought. He has to.

A sour-faced, redheaded woman, awash with freckles, came out of the mourner's tent. Her forehead seemed incised with a perpetual frown, her thin mouth turned down in a crescent. She wore a black *abaya*, with a black scarf placed loosely over her hair, spilling down her back. She perched on a low stool with a rush seat in the shade of the sheik's tent, crossed her arms, and tried to catch Klaus' eye.

"Your friend Gerta Kuntze," Lily said to Klaus, indicating the redheaded woman with a lift of her chin.

"I don't know her."

Behind Klaus, Hamud shook his head, clicked his tongue, and winked an eye. Klaus was lying.

Hamud leaned forward and whispered in Lily's ear. "Look at her. She's a devil. Hair is the color of flames, fly specks all over her skin, and her eyes. Green and cold as stone, like I told you."

The man with the brown turban whom Lily had seen in the Wadi Rum squatted next to the redheaded woman and they began to talk, sitting so close that the sweeping gestures of their arms and hands almost tangled. Gerta Kuntze seemed to glance toward Klaus, no more than the flick of an eye.

Klaus rose. "I've heard of Gerta Kuntze, of course," he said. "She's what my grandfather used to call a *topf-loefel*, a pot stirrer."

Without even a nod to Lily, he strolled away, out toward the desert.

Lily looked back at Gerta Kuntze. The man with the brown turban was gone.

◇◇◇

The judges were ready for the *bisha'a*.

They sat in the shade of the sheik's tent around an open fire, the *mubesha* in charge—a Howeitat elder—on one side, with Gideon next to him. Three judges were seated on the far side of the fire, with Khaled ibn Achmad facing them. A long-handled pan was heating on the embers.

The rest of the witnesses sat under the open flap of the tent. Hamud was among them, but Lily didn't see Klaus anywhere.

The *mubesha* stirred the pan in the fire while he talked in a low voice to Gideon. The pan was almost red hot.

Lily sat cross-legged on the ground away from the others. She was alone at first. Then the redheaded woman squatted next to her.

The woman held out a hand. "Gerta Kuntze." She gave Lily's hand a vigorous shake. "You are the sister of el Tanib?"

Lily nodded.

All the while, the *mubesha* stirred the pan in the fire, taking it out red hot, blowing away the ash, putting it back in the fire to heat again, talking, talking, as he watched Gideon's face.

Gideon's eyes were large with terror. He sat with his hands folded, his cheeks puffy, his lips distended. The pebbles? The *laban*? Would it work?

"Your friend is gone?" Gerta Kuntze asked.

She means Klaus? "It seems so. Would you like to speak with him?"

"No, no. Just asking." Gerta gestured toward the mourner's tent. "Terrible thing, that. In Iraq, under Rashid Ali, such things were not allowed to happen. But here…" Her voice trailed off and she swept her arm around toward the west, indicating the desert, the hills, and for all Lily knew, all of Trans-Jordan. "They let the British take over with their lax British ways. No discipline. No order."

So she admired Rashid Ali, the former Prime Minister, the Nazi sympathizer, the man who led the insurrection and plot against young King Faisal, the man who fled to Berlin when Glubb invaded Iraq. What was Klaus doing with her?

Gerta looked pointedly at Jalil. "And now the British think they can do the same to Iraq." A faint wind shifted the scarf on her head and she adjusted it. "We won't have it. For the sake of Iraq, we won't let it happen." She held out her hand again. "Tell that to your British friends."

She gave Lily's hand a firm shake. "I bid you good day," she said, and went back toward the mourner's tent, while Lily watched the *mubesha* continue his preparations while watching Gideon.

A man detached himself from the Bedouin seated across from the elders, and squatted next to Lily. She looked closer, then recognized him as the man with the straw-colored hair from the sidewalk café. He wore a long white shirt and a voluminous blue cloak. A white *kafiya* covered his straw-like hair, and he had grown a mangy stubble of a beard the color of an old penny. Instead of the curved Bedouin dagger, he wore a knife with a steel handle jammed into a leather scabbard in his belt.

No matter what he did, he couldn't be mistaken for a Bedouin.

The *mubesha* kept the pan on the fire, talking while Gideon nodded.

"In Amman, you ignored my offer," the man with the straw colored hair said.

He moved closer. "That was a mistake."

Lily felt her skin crawl. She shifted away from him, still watching the *mubesha* and Gideon.

"You will live to regret it." The man stood up. "Soon. When you least expect it. You will find out what it means to ignore me."

He turned and went back toward the mourner's tent.

Now the elder cleared his throat and said to Gideon, "We do the fire test." He leaned forward expectantly. The others around him did the same. "There is no way back from the fire test. You understand?"

Gideon nodded. The elder spilled some water from an *ibrit* into the hot pan. Gideon flinched at the sizzling sound of water hitting the hot pan, and nodded again. The elder spilled the water from the pan onto the sand and put the pan back on the fire to heat again.

"You understand what to do," the elder said. "You will lick the pan three times with your tongue, moving your head neither to the right nor to the left." He instructed Gideon by licking his own hand three times. "Then you will rinse your mouth with water three times. The third time you will hold the water in your mouth longer."

Again, Gideon nodded, stiff with fear, his nostrils dilating with each breath.

It will blister, Lily thought, become infected. Please don't let it blister. Don't let Gideon die in pain from gangrene, from an amputated tongue.

Klaus had returned. He squatted among the men by the sheik's tent next to Hamud.

"If the pan leaves a mark," the elder said, "or a burn or swelling, then we know you lie. If your tongue is clean, then you are innocent."

"May Allah help us do justice." The elder called to all assembled to witness the test of fire, and reached for the red-hot pan. He shook off the ash lightly from the bottom with his fingers and held it straight up before Gideon. The crowd waited, sat silent, watched.

Three times Gideon licked the pan without moving his head to the right or the left; and three times he rinsed his mouth with water from the ibrit, holding the water from last rinse in his mouth for a longer time.

"Show me your tongue." The elder inspected Gideon's mouth, grasped Gideon's chin and moved his jaw from side to side.

He showed no expression of the outcome, neither a smile nor a frown, nor the flicker of an eye.

"Show the judges."

The elder sat silently, clasped his hands, bowed his head. Gideon went around the fire and showed his tongue to each of the judges.

Lily continued to hold her breath.

"We are all witnesses," the elder called out, raising both arms above his head. "The man is innocent."

Khaled ibn Achmad jumped up, his face red and hard as a sandstone wall, and shook his fist. "How can that be? Do it again."

"He is telling the truth." The elder said, his look rigid. "There is no other way. The *bisha'a* is final."

"Ignore him," Jalil told Gideon. "He is so ignorant, he can't sort the wheat from the lentils."

But Khaled's nostrils flared as he drew in a deep breath and fixed Gideon with the rancorous eyes of a snake whose split tongue spit fire.

Chapter Twelve

Jalil and Gideon thanked the elders and said goodbye with florid waving of arms and elaborate bows, and Klaus' hand caught in the neck of Hamud's shirt as they rose to leave.

The *bisha'a* was over. The decision was final. Gideon was officially cleared of killing Qasim.

But Lily still wondered who would want Qasim dead? And why? The man with the brown turban? Lily had spotted him watching them in the Wadi Rum before he turned up here at the trial. Did Qasim's death have something to do with the Rashidi? Something to do with the message that Qasim had tried to give Gideon as the wind carried it away?

Someone had killed him with a knife, but every Bedouin in the desert carries a knife. Even Qasim. Qasim's knife was distinctive, with a tooled leather handle and sheath. Klaus had a folding knife with a long blade and a stag handle.

Jalil led the way down the slope as they trudged toward the cars. All but Klaus, who had disappeared again, this time into the mourners' tent.

"I see you met Gerta Kuntze," Jalil said to Lily.

"The Empress of Mesopotamia?"

"She's no el Khatan. She doesn't travel like Gertrude Bell with servants and bathtubs and silver service and Paris gowns."

"What does she travel with?"

"She travels with cases of Mausers, German rifles. Passes them out like candy."

"And that's how she goes from camp to camp as a welcome guest in Bedouin tents?"

"It works for her."

Laughing, Jalil continued down the slope. He told them that they had to go to Azraq, the oasis in the eastern desert. "*Azraq* means blue," he said. "And the oasis is blue with water." He said they had to meet with Colonel Glubb. He called him Abu Huniak.

"There are rumors," Jalil said, "of infiltration from Syria."

On the gradient, Lily's foot glanced off a rock. She skidded along the incline, almost lost her footing, threw out her arms to gain her balance and collided with Hamud.

He cried out, screaming "Scorpion," and began tearing at his cloak, trying to pull it off.

Lily stood back, astonished, wondering what she had done.

Hamud fell to the ground, rolled onto his back, and writhed on the rocky slope, still screaming. He roared in Arabic, his voice heavy with pain as Jalil ran back to him, shouting for help. Screaming, Hamud gripped Jalil's leg and pulled him closer, beseeching Jalil in a coarse whisper as he struggled.

Jalil bent down, to grip his shoulder. "Scorpion bit him on the back," Jalil said. "Inside his cloak." He dragged Hamud to his feet.

Gently peeling off Hamud's cloak, first from one side, then the other, he shook the cloth and tossed the scorpion to the ground. Jalil stomped on it with his sandal, again and again, until it was ground into the sand.

"Whoever the scorpion bites will reach the grave," Hamud said, as if fate had decreed his death. He clutched at Jalil's arm.

"He wants to go back to his people." Jalil led the ashen, shivering Hamud to the Buick and eased him inside.

Jalil started the motor, called out to Gideon to meet him in Azraq, and took off in the direction of Amman.

Klaus still seemed to be in the mourners' tent when Lily and Gideon arrived at the Jeep. They waited. Gideon reached into the Jeep, sounded the horn, and they waited longer.

Lily looked back again at the encampment. Nothing. Klaus was nowhere in sight; she saw only an empty matchbox dancing in the wind along the slope.

Lily and Gideon carefully examined below the seat for scorpions before getting in. Gideon leaned on the horn, shrugged, and tapped the steering wheel impatiently.

"Klaus is gone again." Gideon started the engine, attacked the horn once more, waited, gunned the motor.

"Let him walk." Gideon finally put the Jeep in gear and drove off without Klaus, heading eastward into the measureless silence of the desert.

◇◇◇

They traveled over rolling, flint strewn hills.

Once, the noise of the Jeep roused a herd of gazelle that danced gracefully from crag to crag.

Gideon declared, "Behold, he cometh, leaping upon the mountains, skipping upon the hills. My beloved is like a gazelle or a young hart."

"That's from the Song of Solomon, isn't it?"

Gideon nodded.

"It seems odd to me that something so sensual, so full of sexual desire, would be in the Bible," Lily said.

"There's a lot in the Bible. Incest. Adultery. Murder. Most of all, love." He gave her a sidelong glance. "And lust."

"You mean it's a porno book, not a religious tract?"

"It's the human story. Everything is there. Cain against Abel; Sarah against Hagar; David with all his flaws, and his whole dysfunctional family. And love. Jacob and Rachel, Abraham and Sarah...it echoes the human condition, exposes the human soul."

They watched the gazelles disappear, passing silently behind the hills like ghosts.

The Bible as ethnography, Lily thought. It fits. There's an origin myth, genealogies, legal rules, and case studies.

They rode along without speaking, eastward along the ancient track that led from Qusayr Amra to Azraq, the only sounds the whine of the motor and the clink of tools in the back of the Jeep as it bumped along the rutted terrain.

"What are we really doing here?" Lily asked.

"In Trans-Jordan? Observing the area, gathering information about the terrain, doing reconnaissance. And a little archaeology on the side."

"We're winning the war here?"

"Everything counts. If we don't defeat the Nazis, there is no future."

Lily had seen the future and what it could be. She and Rafi had stopped in New York on the way back from Jerusalem in 1938 and spent a few extra days at the World's Fair. It was called The World of Tomorrow, all blue and white with fountains everywhere. The trylon and the perisphere as white as clouds, the guides dressed in uniforms as blue as the sky. Lily and Rafi had been interviewed at one exhibit, and the interview had been transmitted, voice, moving picture, and all, to a small glass screen that the interviewer called a "television set" in the next room.

She had spoken to a robot, and the robot had answered in a strange mechanical voice. They had watched the American world of tomorrow from a moving chair, magnificent cities strung along miraculous highways like pearls on a string.

They talked about how they would live in a plastic house with a Bakelite telephone and a Plexiglas table, where machines would wash the dishes, clean the house, turn on the lights, and robots would drink milk and answer the telephone. And then, before the fair was over, the future cracked.

The war began and Rafi left. All of it shattered in a fusillade that killed Rafi at El Alamein. For the two of them, there would be no sleek highways, no futuristic cars, no shopping centers that sold shining nylon dresses.

"And Azraq?" she asked. "What are we doing there?"

"Waiting for Glubb."

They drove through a valley surrounded by more solitary cliffs and rocky outcrops, over ground covered with scatters of flint. They bounced over bare earth, the gasoline smell of the engine occasionally yielding to the sharp scent of wormwood and dwarfed tamarisk trees that sprouted in the wadis. Here and there, ahead of them, cinder-cones, stood as reminders of small, long dead volcanoes. Along the track, occasional basalt boulders blocked the path. They had to drive around the rough, broken surface, and Lily wondered what it was like the day a volcano erupted, with unwary creatures slithering through the underbrush and angry magma spewing from the bowels of a restless earth.

Once, Gideon pointed toward a stepped dam in a wadi. "Over there, you see it? The Nabateans built that dam and farmed the desert."

As they drove on, Lily saw the glint of metal against a limestone cliff to the south.

"Look there," she said. "Stop."

Gideon squinted where she pointed. "A piece of corrugated tin. Could be covering the entrance to a cave."

"You think it's a tomb?"

"Not likely."

"Then what is it?"

"Could be natural. Could be used for storage."

"What kind of storage?"

"Sheepskin? Tools?" He shrugged. "Guns?"

"We have to check," she said, and he turned the Jeep toward the cliff.

<>◇<>

Lily removed the overburden from the corrugated tin with her trowel, using a few deft flicks of her wrist.

"You do that very well," Gideon told her.

"Years of experience," she smiled, remembering the first time she had used a trowel.

It was at an Indian site in downstate Illinois, a WPA project. They told her to show up with a Marshalltown trowel, heavy boots, a hat to keep off the sun, a notebook, graph paper, and an indelible pencil. The next day she went back to the hardware store for a line level, a plumb bob, a T-square, and measuring tape.

"It's a three dimensional jigsaw puzzle," the principal investigator had said. "Everything must be measured and recorded in three dimensions from the data point over there." He pointed to a heavy rebar anchored in a concrete slab. "We take it apart here and put it back together in the lab."

The site report was a shock and a disappointment. It had nothing but empty statistics and measurements, graphs looking like battleship curves representing the early presence of an artifact, its rise in popularity, and then its replacement by another, never the reason that it was replaced. The report was about pots, and ignored the potters. There was nothing about what life was like for the Indians, in a world with only stone and fire and clay, life in a lodge dug partly into the ground. None of it was in the site report. It was nothing but a sterile laundry list.

The director of the site declared proudly, "No speculation. This is science, not science fiction. Just the facts. Just the chronology."

Gideon lifted the piece of metal she freed from the opening. "Looks like something from a tin roof. Wonder where they got it."

Lily slid the trowel into her pocket and leaned forward. "Look. It's a man-made opening. Here are the cut marks, made with a metal tool, a chisel, or a pickaxe."

She stood up to let Gideon peer inside.

"I can see gouges from a chisel on the ceiling. There's something in there. Could be a cache of some kind. Hard to tell. Pretty deep, over six feet." He pressed closer, then stood up grinning. "I can't fit through the opening. Bedouin are smaller than me."

Lily bent down again in the entrance. In the eerie gray light of the cave, she could just make out the cut marks from the chisel used to hollow it out from the limestone hillside. It was deep but not large, maybe two meters from the entrance to the back of the cave, and three meters across.

"It's a hand-hewn cave," she said. "Bedouin don't bury like this. Could this be a tomb anyway?"

"More likely used for storage. This limestone is friable and easy to work. It hardens after it's exposed to air for a while and dries out."

She leaned in farther. "I can fit through."

"You want to try it?"

"How?"

"Tie a rope around you like a harness. I'll lower you down."

"Carefully."

Chapter Thirteen

Gideon lowered her into the cave, releasing the tension slowly on the rope. She had taken off her new hat and wriggled through the opening, head first, then splayed out her hands on the floor of the cave before she righted herself to sit on the uneven surface.

Something had been stored here. Now silt covered whatever had been stowed.

She scraped with her trowel. Working with it raised dust. She coughed a little and kept scraping. The air, thick and heavy, weighed her down, but she kept moving the trowel back and forth, raising more dust.

She tried to take a breath, heaving her shoulders, and coughed instead.

There's no air in here. She scratched away more silt.

I can't breathe. The silt covered her hands, her sleeves, her sandals.

What was it Jalil said inhabited caves? A ghula, an evil witch.

She gasped, wheezed, used all her strength to take a breath. *I can't breathe.*

"Gideon, pull me up. I can't breathe."

He didn't answer. He's there. She heard a stirring outside, but he didn't answer.

"I can't breathe." She tried to shout and struggled for breath between each word.

The ghula is devouring my soul.

"Gideon. Please."

Air heavy as darkness.

"Gideon, I can't breathe."

She tried to yell out, pulled on the rope to attract his attention.

Someone is out there. He should answer.

The rope went slack, fell loose in her hand.

Where was Gideon?

She called him again. No answer.

Gideon gone. And she was trapped, suffocating in the cave.

Chapter Fourteen

Lily huddled on the floor of the cave, dangling one end of the rope from one hand, shifting the other back and forth in the silt below her.

I've got to get out of here. Rocking back and forth, she rubbed against something bulging from the floor. In the cave's half-twilight, she made out a long strip of wood and metal.

Got to get out of here.

Dust motes bobbed in the shaft of daylight coming from the cave entrance. She shuffled toward the opening, grabbed at the wall, stretched her arms toward the light. She could just reach the edge of the opening.

Pull yourself up. Lean on the ledge and crawl out.

She hooked her fingers around the edge of the opening and strained to pull herself up.

Can't. Too high.

She slumped back to the floor of the cave, breathless again, and began to shiver. So cold in here, she thought.

Got to get out. How?

She put her head between her knees, closed her eyes.

Relax.

She tried a deep breath of the leaden air, then another. She sat back a moment, thought, felt some of the tension leave her shoulders, opened her eyes.

Some kind of traction. Got to get traction.

She rubbed back and forth again against the object bulging from the silt. She looked down, clawed at the dirt around it.

Nothing but a shotgun, an old shotgun with a rusted barrel and a long crack in the wooden handle. What good would it do? *Still no way out.*

She pulled at the shotgun. It moved, exposing a desert scorpion, white and gelatinous, startled by the light, scurrying back toward the darkness beneath the rifle. Instinctively, she picked up the trowel, smashed the scorpion with the sharp edge, cut it in half. The entrails of the scorpion squirted on her hand, her sleeve, her cheek. She wiped it off, crouched on the floor, and began to shiver again.

Her reaction to the scorpion had been swift, almost a reflex. It stunned Lily, reminded her that she had a reserve of courage that she could tap.

She focused on the wall, the opening where light flooded in, hot and bright. She thought of the holes gouged into the rock at Petra as footholds for workmen.

She looked back at the shotgun.

Now she could use it.

She cleaned the trowel in the silt, used it to loosen the dirt around the shotgun and tugged at it. She could hardly lift it. Picking up the barrel with both hands, using all her strength, she swung it around, knocking the butt against the wall of the cave. A large flake spalled off the wall, leaving a white scar in the limestone. A narrow notch, enough for a foothold? Barely deep enough for a toe.

The flake that came off looked like an oversized scraper with a bulb of percussion and force lines radiating from it—an enormous clamshell with a pronounced hinge. She picked it up to snap off a piece. It crumbled. Was the wall of the cave that friable?

She picked up the trowel and gouged out a deeper notch. *One foothold, one to go.*

She swung the rifle again as hard as she could, knocked off a flake eighteen inches above the other, stood back, dug into it with the trowel, then shoved the trowel into the belt of her jodhpur.

One end of the rope was still tied around her waist. She secured the loose end to the shotgun and went back to the opening. Standing on tiptoe, she thrust the rifle through, barrel first. She rested, breathless from exertion. Then she pushed until the butt of the shotgun was outside the cave. She turned the gun, paused to breathe, and kept edging it around until it rested against the entrance, parallel to the ground and anchored against the sides of the opening.

She yanked at the rope. A scattering of small limestone flakes rained down, but the rope held.

She put one foot in the first toehold, stepped up. The edge of the foothold gave way. She slipped, dropped the trowel, fell to the ground, the breath knocked out of her. Her elbow hit the edge of the trowel, and she gasped.

Not again. Damn, damn, damn. This isn't going to work.

She panted, short frightened breaths. After a minute, she relaxed, inhaled. Just winded from the fall. She still held the rope. She pulled herself to a sitting position, fingered the sting in her arm where the trowel had cut her. She was bleeding.

Tugging at the rope, she stood up and tried again. This time, she worked upward, hand over hand, swaying like a pendulum, moving up the rope, stopping for breath, sliding down, the rope burning her hands, moving up again.

Almost at the entrance.

At last, the heat of the sun penetrating from outside. She knocked her wrist against the shotgun and clung to it, ignoring the blisters forming on her hands.

She pulled herself up, crawled out of the cave.

Outside, she caught sight of a Bedouin fleeing over the hill, his cloak flying in the wind. Gideon lay on the ground, groaning, clutching the back of his head.

"You all right?"

"I have a headache," he said.

"What happened?"

"I'm not sure. Someone hit me. My head hurts."

"You said that. Who was it? Khaled?"

"I don't know. He attacked from behind. The next thing I knew, he started running away when he saw the gun you stuck out of the cave. I must have passed out. I have a headache." He sat up. "And now I'm dizzy."

"Maybe you have a concussion. You sick to your stomach?"

"No, no. I'm fine. Just a headache."

With a concussion, Lily knew, people are disoriented, repeat themselves, have problems with vision.

Lily held up two fingers. "How many fingers am I holding up?"

"My God, you're bleeding. Did he hit you too?"

"No. How many fingers?"

"Two. I'm all right. I just have a headache. And a bump on the back of my head." He raised his hand to rub it again. "It's going to swell up. You have an icepack handy?"

"Very funny."

"I told you I'm all right." He tried to smile and reached into his pocket for the keys to the Jeep. "You drive. I'm a little tired. And I have a headache."

She hoisted the rusty shotgun, wrapped the rope around it, and bundled it into the back of the Jeep while Gideon watched.

"Looks like it was left over from the last war. Lawrence passed by here." He handed her the keys. "Just follow the track to Azraq. Can't miss it."

He trudged over to the Jeep, got in the passenger seat, closed his eyes, and fell asleep.

Chapter Fifteen

"You all right?" Lily asked as Gideon opened his eyes and rubbed the back of his head. "We're in Azraq."

"The headache's a little better. But I've got a bump back here the size of Cleveland."

Lily scanned the oasis, the springs, water, waving date palms, herds of gazelle, and flocks of birds.

Gideon pointed to a somber squat building of black basalt. "That's the British military hospital."

Lily drove to the front of the building. "Let them have a look at you."

"I'm all right." He tossed his head with an air of bravado and winced.

He was frightened, Lily thought, under the veneer of courage, of fortitude and independence.

She drove to the shade of the building and turned off the motor. She helped Gideon out of the Jeep and moved him carefully toward the heavy basalt door of the hospital.

He eyed the cut on her arm. "You coming in?"

She pulled open the door with her blistered hand and winced.

They waited at a counter in the hospital corridor that smelled faintly of chlorine and ether and rotting flesh, and took in the whitewashed walls, the black and white tile floor. After a while, an orderly gave them a quizzical look.

"You want the surgery?" he asked, and led them down the hall to a doctor.

They emerged an hour later, having been told to take two aspirin and come back in the morning.

Lily sported adhesive plasters on her palms, orange Mercurochrome painted on her arm, and a butterfly bandage pulling together the edges of her cut. Gideon clasped an icepack to the back of his head.

"You're really all right?" Lily asked.

"Of course I am. I told you."

"No more headache?"

"Almost gone."

"Still sleepy?"

He shook his head, winced a little, then waved an arm at Azraq, as if the oasis was his personal gift. "Beautiful, isn't it?"

She gazed at the calm blue pools of water which reflected the flocks of birds hovering over them, calling, flapping wings, circling in live eddies of motion and sound.

"This is where early man hunted, this is where Romans camped, where their emperors built a fort. This is Eden. What more could anyone want?"

Lily wanted Rafi back. She wanted a big old house that creaked and sighed in the night like tired lovers. When she was a girl, when she visited her grandmother on Long Island in the summer, she would walk down to the beach along a cracked sidewalk edged with sand. She would stop at an old abandoned house with a widow's-walk along the roof that faced the sea, with outbuildings, with weathervanes, with shuttered windows and a garden cluttered with leaves from ancient trees, and imagine living there. At the curb, a concrete step said *Mon Terrace*. For mounting horses, she supposed, maybe a carriage step. She wanted to live in this house, full of little boys, so she could play their mother.

I still want a house with groaning wooden floors and children's feet clattering on the stairs, she thought, and I want Rafi reading a book under a lamp, not blown apart at El Alamein in the Western Desert.

"I want a bath," she said. "I want to soak in a tub of hot water and then I want to sleep for a day and a half on a feather bed with a box springs mattress and then I want another bath. I want to win the war. Beyond that, I just don't know."

"If a hot bath is the highest human aspiration," Gideon said, "then God is weeping."

Chapter Sixteen

Two Bedouin and a Druze with a rounded white hat and trim beard stood at the edge of the saltpan. Beyond them, the blue pools of Azraq shimmered in haze from the heat. The fort, built of basalt, strangely dark and medieval, spread out behind the pools.

Next to the pan, a collection of black goat-haired tents surrounded a large white marquee with the sides pulled up to catch the late afternoon breeze.

"That's Sheik Suleimon." Gideon gestured toward an old man propped against pillows in the shade of the white marquee, his jaw slack in sleep. "Came here for the salt."

Lily had heard of Sheik Suleimon, famous for his wealth; the extent of his progeny, almost a thousand and counting; and his penchant for women, especially blondes. It was said that Sheik Suleimon once spotted a beautiful young woman at a camel market, asked to arrange a marriage, and was told that it was impossible, that she was his granddaughter. It was said that he had placed ads in personal columns of British and German newspapers, looking for blond wives; that he offered ten-thousand dollars bride price; that he had accumulated more than the four wives allotted in the Moslem tradition. It was said that in his youth, he was handsome and charismatic, the inspiration for Rudolph Valentino's films about the Sheik of Araby.

With a tilt of his head, Gideon indicated the Bedouin at the saltpan who had started toward them. "We're in for some desert hospitality."

"You want to meet Sheik Suleimon?" he asked Lily. "He'll invite us to eat and to spend the night."

The Bedouin bowed with a sweep of his cloak, asked about Gideon's health, and invited him to the sheik's tent. "Just some coffee," the Bedouin had said, "and perhaps a bit of bread to speed you on your way."

Gideon answered that he must hurry, that he must spend the night in the fort to meet with Abu Huniak.

"Just a little water." But the sheik had already ordered his men to kill a goat, and now it was evening and they awaited a Bedouin feast in the white tent. The tent was large, the flaps closed against the cool night air, the ground and sides covered with fine silk carpets. Gideon and the two Bedouin from the saltpan sat on one side of the tent and Lily sat alone on the opposite side.

Sheik Suleimon leaned back in a pillow-covered chair on a platform at the far end of the tent, his eyes closed. He had a white *kafiya* wrapped around his head, with a gold-decorated *egal,* the cord that holds a *kafiya* in place. He wore an embroidered tunic over a long white shirt, over that a cloak, and over that another cloak, as well as a shawl across his shoulders. Two middle-aged Bedouin sat cross-legged on cushions on either side of him.

At last, a boy appeared, carrying a tiered brass stand that held a basin of water and a tray with soap and a towel. The boy left after they finished washing their hands, and returned with an enormous copper tray—a *seniyah*—piled high with meat and rice atop a layer of flat Bedouin bread. He placed it in front of Gideon. On the very top of the mound of food, and facing Gideon, was the boiled head of a goat and a pair of goat's eyes, delicacies reserved for an honored guest.

Gideon blinked.

The boy returned again with a smaller *seniyah* that he placed in front of Lily. Her seniyah held the neck bones of the goat, the part next to the head, a singular honor for a woman. The next time she glanced toward Gideon, she saw that the goat's eyeballs had disappeared. Had he eaten them? Had he palmed them?

She watched Gideon and the Bedouin eat, tearing off chunks of the bread, rolling it around meat and rice, and she did the same, using her right hand, only her right hand. The left, she knew, was just for washing.

The old sheik opened his eyes and squinted at her. She remembered to lower her own, not to stare, to look modest. Eye contact was brazen, vulgar in a woman.

The sheik stirred in his chair and said something to one of the younger men seated next to him. The man helped him to stand, step down from the platform, and approach Lily.

Braced by the Bedouin who held his arm, the old man bent down and peered at her with rheumy eyes clouded by cataracts. A network of wrinkles scored his face. He mumbled to his companion and his trim white beard moved with his words. Lily wasn't sure what she should do. She kept eating, her eyes fixed on the food in front of her.

Did the sheik think that Gideon and she visited to arrange a marriage? She looked down at the *seniyah* and felt her face flush.

The old sheik muttered again, and the Bedouin led him back to his chair, one careful step at a time, the old man open-mouthed, gasping for shreds of air.

How much would he offer Gideon as bride price, Lily wondered? Fifty pounds? Twenty pounds? A camel and a goat?

⟨⟩⟨⟩⟨⟩

Lily leaned back, feeling that she had overeaten. Opposite her, Gideon had done the same.

"Wonderful meal, wonderful," he said. "I couldn't eat another morsel."

The boy reappeared, this time with a basin of water and soap and a warm wet towel to wipe their hands and faces. As they left, the old man stood at the door of the tent and bowed them out, with a special low bow for Lily, gesturing that his heart, his mouth, his head, were at her disposal. Again, she blushed and lowered her eyes.

"No offer of marriage?" Lily asked Gideon after they left.

"Tomorrow. It's rude to discuss business in the tent."

"Business?"

"For you," Gideon said, "it would involve high finance."

<><><>

They spent that night in the black basalt fort. Klaus was waiting for them outside the fort. The Bedouin with the brown turban from Wadi Rum, with a mangy dog scratching a tawny coat, stood near him.

"I found someone to be our guide." Klaus pointed to the Bedouin, a small man with the air of a bantam cock. He swaggered toward them, his hand on the hilt of a dagger in a scabbard decorated with small glass bicycle reflectors.

"He knows the area," Klaus told them. "Says he knows of some archaeological sites around here."

"Where did he come from?" Gideon asked. "I didn't see anyone on our way in."

"There's a small Ruwalla encampment not far from here in the wadi. This is Ibrahim ibn Rashid."

Lily wondered how Klaus knew of the Ruwalla encampment.

"This is your dog?" she asked the Bedouin.

"He follows me."

He picked up a stone and pitched it at the dog, hitting it on the flank. The dog yelped, whined and scurried behind a rock. "Sometimes, he helps me hunt."

Ibrahim ibn Rashid watched the dog slink away, gave Gideon a grudging bow, glanced over at Lily, then gestured toward Klaus. "He says you will pay."

Gideon looked surprised. Someone official had usually arranged for a guide—General Donovan or Emir Abdullah.

He reached into his pocket for his wallet. "Of course." He fished out a half-pound note and handed it to Ibrahim.

"This is just a piece of paper." Ibrahim inspected it and turned it over. "With a picture of a Hashemite. It is worthless to me."

"What do you want?" Gideon asked him.

"A goat. A donkey. A camel."

"With this note, you can buy a goat."

"Where?"

"In Karak, in Amman."

"How would I get there? This piece of paper is worthless to me." He tore the note in half and threw it on the ground.

Gideon bent down to pick up the torn note and glared at Klaus.

"He's just a Bedouin," Klaus said. "He only knows the desert, but he knows it well." He turned to Ibrahim. "We will get you a goat."

<><><>

Lily dreamed of Rafi again the next evening and couldn't get back to sleep.

She strolled around the periphery of the pool near the fort, breathing in the sensuous, silent beauty of the desert. In the silver moonlight, the eerie outline of boulders cast deep shadows.

Gideon stood on the verge of the pool, gazing across its surface, the quiet ripples sparkling and pale blue in the night.

"I couldn't sleep," she told him.

"Bad dreams?"

She nodded.

They walked along the ancient shoreline, slowly savoring the night perfume of the desert, the sharp odor of wormwood, of terebinth, and gazed up at the velvet sky, bejeweled with stars.

"The ancient Babylonians," Lily said, "thought every star was a god, that the gods lived up there in the sky in a world of their own."

"Look there." She pointed skyward. "A falling star." They watched as it crossed the sky and disappeared.

Gideon turned to her and smiled. "Another Babylonian god bites the dust."

"It didn't even leave a track. A god is missing, and there's nothing left to mark its place."

"Like in your bad dream?" Gideon gazed at her. "Brightness that passed through your life and left no trace?"

"Maybe." She turned her face away to tell him about Rafi, of their broken plans, of his last moments at El Alamein, how he was caught in the crossfire in a German minefield.

"He didn't have time to live." Her voice caught. "He left nothing behind. No child, no family, no heritage."

"There's always your memory of him."

"And then what? Nothing else to show that he ever lived."

Gideon took a deep breath and put his hands in his pockets. He looked up at the stars again, each one a god going about his business, winking at him before moving on.

"You think that has anything to do with what happened to you in the cave yesterday?"

He watched her, waiting for her reaction. She stared at him, blank-faced.

"In Hebrew, the root for the word for tomb is the same as that for cave."

"I dug in caves before. Tombs as well, with never a problem."

"I know that. The tombs at Tel el Kharub. Eastbourne, direc-tor of the site, was killed. And the cave in Morocco. That time, it was Drury who was murdered."

Lily felt a chill. "Getting cold out here."

"You think so?"

She clasped her arms tight across her chest.

"When did you last see Rafi?" Gideon asked.

"In Chicago, before he left. Over a year ago. Almost two years."

"When did you find out what happened?"

"Last November."

He took his hands out of his pockets and looked over at her. "It takes a year, two sometimes, to recover from a loss. Everyone must grieve in their own way, take their own time. Rituals are important, like the one at the mourner's tent we saw at the Bedouin encampment. You had none."

"You learned all this in your course on grief counseling at the seminary?"

"Something like that."

"You sound wise, but you don't know how it feels. I still have regrets."

"A life without regrets is a life not lived."

She shook her head. "Don't give me platitudes. That's not it. We neglected time. We thought we had all the time in the world."

She blinked back the sting of tears, and shivered. "I'd best be getting back. Even with stars, it's cold here."

Chapter Seventeen

In the cool of the morning at first light, Lily, Klaus, and Ibrahim loaded the Jeep outside the fort before they went out into the desert for a day's reconnaissance.

Klaus continued to pontificate on Ibrahim's virtues, emphasizing that the Ruwalla knew of caves and archaeological sites that couldn't be found without his help.

Ibrahim leaned on his rifle, glaring at the fort. He had refused to spend the night inside.

"Was Lawrence's headquarters," he said. "Lawrence lied." He shook his head, spit on the ground. "Lawrence and his friend, al Khatan. Both betrayed us."

"Lawrence wasn't all bad," Lily said, feeling obliged to defend a fellow archaeologist. "He understood the Bedouin, lived among you."

"A donkey's a donkey, even if he's raised among horses. He made promises he didn't keep."

"He tried," she said.

Gideon brought out a box filled with bread, hard-boiled eggs, cucumbers, tomatoes, and a jar of feta cheese floating in oil. He set it down beside the jugs of cooled, boiled water, and went back into the fort for more supplies.

Ibrahim hitched the hem of his abaya over his shoulder, rested the carton on it and started toward the Jeep, with his dog sniffing and haunting his footsteps. He dropped the box into the back of the Jeep with a thud, pushed the dog away with his foot, and went back for the water. Lily cringed as the dog whimpered, crept away and lay down on its side in the dirt beyond the Jeep.

Gideon emerged again, grinning this time, carrying a watermelon.

"Where'd you get that?" Lily asked.

"From the icebox in the Legion kitchen."

"You stole it?"

"I only borrowed it."

"So when we finish eating it we'll give it back?"

"Some day, I will buy a bigger and better watermelon and dedicate it to the icebox at Azraq."

"Even if it takes forty years?"

"Exactly so," Gideon said, handing off the melon to Ibrahim.

Ibrahim reached for the melon with a smile, thumped it, dumped it on top of the box of food, and climbed into the back of the Jeep.

"Careful, you'll break the water jugs," Lily said.

She rearranged the box and then turned back to Ibrahim to pick up the threads of their old conversation, curious about what he said about Lawrence and Gertrude Bell.

"You don't approve of Gertrude Bell?" she asked.

"She wished to be called al Khatun, the Lady," Ibrahim's nostrils quivered in anger. "She sailed around the desert from tent to tent with a train of camels loaded with chests of linen and silver and dishes, and a bathtub, in fancy dresses and flowered hats, throwing baksheesh to sheiks and camel-drivers. Like a queen."

"I thought all the Bedouin liked her."

"They liked her baksheesh. What can you say of a woman who acts like a man? She was a foolish piece of noise, always talking, always giving orders, a man-woman donkey." He shrugged and wiped his hands together in a gesture of dismissal. "She was in love with Faisal," he added, and Lily was surprised. "Made him king of Iraq."

"Faisal? Grandfather of the present king? Gertrude Bell and Faisal had an affair?"

"*Laa.*" He shook his head and clicked his tongue against his teeth. "No affair. She was too ugly. And I think, what I think, Faisal was in love with Lawrence, and Lawrence was in love with him."

"A *ménage à trois?*"

"What's that?"

"Never mind," Lily said.

"Faisal put up with el Khatan because she was Lawrence's friend," Ibrahim said. "And because she made him King of Iraq." He rubbed at his face and shook his head again, this time in disgust. "Why Iraq? He was stranger. He was from the Hejaz."

He twitched his head. "Now Iraq is ruled by a useless child."

Lily remembered the picture of the curly haired Faisal, looking sad and frightened next to his confident cousin Hussein.

Gideon came out of the fort, carrying two canvas water bags that he hung on either side of the Jeep.

"Ready to go?" He turned to Klaus. "Got your camera, your film?"

They clambered into the loaded Jeep. As Gideon drove out of the fort compound, the dog chased after them, tangling with the wheels, snapping, barking. Gideon gunned the motor, sped away, and left the dog in a wake of whirling dust.

<><><>

Jalil caught up with them by late morning.

The day was heating up. They had paused and rested in the shade of the Jeep, eating chunks of the watermelon, sucking the sweet, sticky juice, letting it run down their chins.

Awadh, the older Bdoul from Petra, was with Jalil. Both rode fine Arabian steeds, shining chestnuts, sleek and proud.

Jalil dismounted. "Brought you a new guide." He indicated the Bdoul.

Awadh's face was vibrant with smiles as he told Lily his new horse was called Ghalib, named for a great warrior.

Ibrahim stood, his hand resting on the hilt of the gaudy dagger at his waist. "He knows nothing. He's an old man."

"He knows a great deal because he's an old man," Jalil said.

Awadh, still beaming, gave a modest nod of his head. "I was with Lawrence."

Ibrahim looked ready to spring at him.

"We can use both," Klaus said. "The more the merrier. I've hired Ibrahim. He's Ruwalla, knows this part of the desert."

Jalil nodded. "*Ahlen we Sahlen*, Welcome in peace." He spoke to Ibrahim, but he looked worried.

"Suleimon is dead," Jalil told them. "And there's been infiltration from Syria. This morning, a Syrian raid at the saltpans. They came for the salt, stole flocks. Killed two men of Suleimon's *khamsa*."

Lily envisioned tribal warfare raging across the desert. "They killed Suleimon?"

"No, no. Heart attack. The tumult of the raid. He was ancient. He's been sick. His men were distracted."

"We were guests for dinner in Suleimon's tent just yesterday." Lily pictured the old sheik who bent over her, squinting at her through clouded eyes. "It's sad."

"We can't count on Suleimon's men now." Jalil looked north. "Their camp is in confusion." He nodded and took a few shallow breaths as if he were sniffing the air. "That's not all. Umm al Quttein was attacked."

"Who attacked? Same raiders?" Gideon asked. "What did they attack?"

"Umm al Quttein is on the south slope of Jebel Druze, just this side of the Syrian border. It's an Arab Legion post, just a few kilometers from pumping station H5. A contingent of Syrians, Germans, Vichy French, and a force of Druze cavalry." He looked north again. "Vichy French officers led the attack."

"H5?" Gideon asked. "On the Kirkuk-Haifa pipeline?"

Jalil nodded. "They're after sabotage. If they blow up the pipeline…"

It was beginning to make sense to Lily now, this wandering through the desert from site to site, even the accidental meeting with Suleimon's encampment.

Jalil paused, wary, watching a man on a camel ride toward them, waving, his cloak flapping as he came over the ridge.

When the man drew closer, Jalil relaxed. "It's Hamud. *Hamdulillah*. May Allah be praised."

Lily gave Hamud a broad smile. "Welcome back. We missed you."

"I thought that whoever the scorpion bites will reach the grave," Klaus said.

"And so I shall," Hamud said, dismounting and couching his camel. "Someday. But not yet."

"Even if it takes forty years?" Lily asked.

"Or more. *Inshallah*. If Allah is willing."

"To what do you owe your good fortune?" Jalil asked, "*Ma'ah hadas?*"

"My people have a cure for the bite." Hamud spread out his hand and extended his fingers.

"First." He pressed down his index finger. "To break the spell of the scorpion, a friend slaughters a neighbor's goat.

"Second." He pressed down his middle finger. "The friend puts the goat innards into the water to wash the bite.

"Then," he turned down the next finger. "The friend digs a grave."

Taking in his breath somberly for a dramatic pause, he looked at each of them in turn. "He carried me to the grave. In a few minutes, he carried me out, and quickly, quickly, put the innards of the goat in my place.

"And the poison was passed to the goat." He opened his hand and flung out his arm, as if to toss away an evil spell. "The spell of the scorpion was broken." He clapped his hands together. "I lived."

"*Hamdulillah*," said Lily.

Jalil nodded in agreement. "*Hamdulillah*," he said, and moved toward his horse. "But for now, we must get back to Azraq, check on H5 and make preparations to attack T3."

"What's T3?" Lily asked.

"A pumping station on the pipeline through Syria from Mosel. Feeds oil to the Vichy French and the Germans."

"That means," Gideon said, "that we have to extend our archaeological survey as far north as Palmyra. It's never been adequately excavated."

"Palmyra?" Lily said. "It's in Syria."

"In an oasis in the Great Syrian Desert, on a flat plain covered with desert pavement." He smiled, shrugged and said to Lily, "It's just north of T3."

"The Syrians call it Tadmor," Jalil added. "There's nothing there now, except for a small fort for the French Foreign Legion and the Syrian Camel Corp. That, and a few ugly houses."

Palmyra, Bride of the Desert, an oasis on the road to the riches of the Far East. Zenobia defeated the Romans as queen of Palmyra, one of a long line of fabulous warrior queens that intrigued Lily. Zenobia rode into battle fearless and passionate, hair flowing, breast exposed. Lily sometimes associated the ancient Greek myths of the Amazons with this tradition of warrior queens.

Palmyra was near the T3 pumping station of the pipeline that led through Syria. It made sense. They were here because of the pipelines, one that led through Trans-Jordan to Haifa that supplied the British with oil, the other that ran through Nazi controlled Syria and supplied the Axis.

But there was more to it than that. They kept moving toward Iraq, the Iraq governed by a child who had inherited the throne through the machinations of the romantic, manipulative British heiress, al Khatun.

Iraq oil held the balance that fed the campaigns of the British and the Axis. And the linchpin was a sad-eyed child.

Rashid Ali was in exile in Berlin, Glubb had said. But suppose he was in Syria?

Lily put her hand on Gideon's arm. "I'll go with you, of course."

"It could be dangerous."

"I'll watch your back."

"I don't know." Gideon smiled and shook his head. "You don't have a very good track record watching people's backs.

Eastbourne in Tel el Kurnub, Drury in Tangier, both killed. If it happens a third time, you've established a trend."

"We'd better get going," Jalil helped them pack up, mounted his horse, and led the motley procession as it turned back to Azraq, with Jalil and Awadh on horseback, Hamud on his camel, and the others in the Jeep.

At the fort, Gideon parked and started toward the gate, then bent down to pick up something from the ground.

"What is it?" Lily asked.

"Looks like Qasim's knife." He held out a knife with a tooled black leather handle and sheath. "How did it get here? He had it with him in Wadi Rum."

Lily shuddered. "Whoever killed Qasim and took his knife is with us, here in Azraq."

The others arrived one by one and busied themselves watering and hobbling the animals, hitching the horses, couching the camel.

Ibrahim watched them trudge inside. "Lies beget lies," he said. "Betrayal begets betrayal."

In the morning, he was gone. The rusted shotgun with the broken barrel from World War I and the training rifle Jalil had brought for Lily were gone with him.

Chapter Eighteen

Today it was just the three of them on their way to check on the pumping station at H5. They were prepared for the day like Boy Scouts, with canteens filled, canvas water bags hanging from the sides of the Jeep, sandwiches in a cooler in the back.

Gideon drove east between the black lava hills along the Haifa-Baghdad road, with Lily in the passenger seat. Great lava boulders lined the road, hulking sentinels of an ancient volcanic eruption.

Jalil sprawled in the back of the Jeep, gripping a large pair of field glasses like a new toy, taking them from the case, raising them to scan the flint-strewn plain and putting them back.

"Seven times magnification." Jalil patted the binocular case affectionately. "Bausch and Lomb, best make."

He handed Lily the field glasses. "Take a look."

She held them up to adjust the focus. The heavy binoculars banged against her cheek when the Jeep hit a bump, and she focused again.

She held the rubber cups of the field glasses tight against her face, scanning the horizon, watching the dust swirling in their wake, and following the base of the low hills rising on either side.

She spotted the slight dip in the hillside, covered with a slab of basalt.

"Over there." She pointed. "Looks like a cave."

Gideon left the track to turn the Jeep in the direction she was pointing. "Over where?"

She lowered the binoculars. "Keep going straight." The road was rougher now. "You're going in the right direction."

She bounced off the seat, and down again. "For God sake, slow down."

"I see it now," Gideon said.

"What do you see?" Jalil said.

Gideon pointed. "See that piece of basalt against the hill?"

"Yes. So?"

"Could be the entrance to a cave. Could be used to store arms."

Lily got out as soon as they reached the cave. "Smells more like garbage." She pulled the basalt rock away from the small cave entrance.

Inside, the stench was overwhelming.

"Good God! It's Ibrahim's dog." Two steps led down from the entrance. The dog, covered with bugs and slithering maggots, lay half on the edge of the bottom step.

"The training rifle and old shotgun he stole are on the floor of the cave. I better go in."

She lowered herself to shimmy inside the entrance.

"You sure you can so this?" Gideon asked.

She sensed he meant her panic when she was trapped in the cave before they got to Azraq, and was mortified.

"It won't happen again. Not this time, anyway."

"What won't?"

Lily looked over her shoulder at him, smiled, and slid warily into the cave, avoiding the dog, keeping her eyes on the rifle and shotgun. For a moment, she glanced toward the dog, gagged, and turned away. It won't happen again, she told herself.

She reached the floor and carefully lifted the shotgun through the entrance to Gideon outside, then reached for the rifle, ready to crawl up the steps. Holding the gun in both hands, she stretched up toward the entrance, pushed the butt of the rifle through, and lost her balance.

She landed on the soft, half putrefied flesh of the dog.

Creatures moved along her arm, crawled along her neck, crept inside her shirt. She leaped up the steps, scrambled through the opening, and came out screaming.

She ripped off her shirt and stomped on it, slapping insects and maggots off her arms. Still screaming, she wriggled out of her slacks and stomped on them with her feet, hearing the crunch of the insects, stamping, shouting, "Go away, go away, go away."

Brushing her arms and legs again, she paused to lift the stone with both hands and heave it onto the clothes and quivering vermin on the ground. She jumped on it and collapsed, cross-legged, on the ground, weeping.

Gideon brought a canteen and spilled water over her hands. "Here." He handed her the canteen.

She poured the water over her head and down her shoulders, rubbing at her arms and legs, brushing more insects into the dust. They crawled out of the sun. "What are those things?"

"Maggots?"

"The other things, those dark, hairy bugs."

"Dermestids. They're beetles. Some people call them cemetery beetles." He went back to the jeep and fished for a towel. "They clean up putrefying flesh."

"They were eating the dog?"

"They eat carrion. Keep our cemeteries tidy and hygienic."

"If cemeteries are such healthy places," Lily mumbled, "why aren't the dead out playing tennis?"

She rubbed herself vigorously with the towel, shook it out, rubbed and shook again. "They could eat me." She stood up. "I could go to sleep tonight and in the morning I could wake up dead, nothing but a skeleton."

"They only eat decaying flesh."

She flicked off the last insect that she could find, then jumped up and down, shaking, to make strays fall away. "For all I know, I might be decaying."

Gideon looked her figure up and down with a sly smile. "I don't think so." He handed her a fresh shirt and slacks that he had retrieved from the Jeep. "And neither do the Bedouin watching from beyond the ridge."

Jalil stood discreetly with his back turned to her. But beyond him, Lily made out a pair of faint shadows with billowing cloaks at the top of the hill.

Chapter Nineteen

They drove on toward H5, bumping along the track that followed the pipeline, veering occasionally to avoid one of the black boulders scattered across the open plain.

As they approached the pumping station, they heard the noise, like distant thunder, echoing among the hills long before they realized what was happening. Jalil lifted his field glasses, turned his head to sweep the horizon.

Closer to the pumping station, the sound was more distinct, a steady series of blasts muffled, in part, by a wind that blew toward Iraq.

A mile from H5, they pulled to the side of the road, and stood next to the Jeep openmouthed, watching dust and smoke erupt from the ground near the pumping station.

Jalil peered through the field glasses again. "Vichy French fighter." He lowered the binoculars. "He doesn't see us yet."

Squinting, Lily could barely make out the outline of an airplane in the distance, saw it bank and turn, spew red tracer bullets, and leisurely bank again.

"How do you know who it is?" she asked.

"Body painted yellow, with the tricolor roundel near the tail. Glubb gave us photos, silhouettes of planes to identify."

This time, the fighter banked and flew directly at them in a flurry of noise, firing, churning fountains of dirt and dust as it came.

"He spotted us," Lily said.

"Quick," Jalil shouted over the roar of the engine, "under the Jeep."

"Shouldn't we make a diversion?" Lily turned her back on the oncoming plane. "Draw him away from H5?"

"He's coming at us. We're the diversion. Get under the Jeep." Gideon grabbed her sleeve. "Now. It's our only cover."

"We could drive in the other direction," Lily still ignored the looming plane. "Slalom around the boulders."

"There's no cover here," Jalil said. "It would be suicide. After he kills us, he'll go back to H5. We'd be dead for no reason."

She looked around at the open field, bare and gray and dusty. "But...."

Gideon grasped her arm. "This is no time to gawk. He's shooting at us. Come on, come on," he shouted.

"We have no anti-aircraft weapons," Jalil said.

"You have rifles."

"Are you crazy?" Jalil asked her. "You can't shoot down a plane with a rifle."

The airplane bore down on them, firing, kicking up columns of dust.

"He's strafing." Jalil turned away. "Under the Jeep. It's our only chance." He disappeared beneath the vehicle.

Finally, she ducked under the running board, and crawled into the oily underbelly of the Jeep.

She heard the fighter climb, bank, come in lower, the shriek of the engine receding, banking, returning again, lower.

The Jeep vibrated, swayed under the strident attack of the plane.

Dust clotted the air. The plane's engines screamed. Its machine-gun chattered.

It banked again, roared lower still, gripping the Jeep under its shadow, shooting a blast of sound, shattering a nearby boulder.

A piece of the boulder rocked the Jeep with the impact. It ripped the canvas water bag hanging from the side, spewing water onto the desert-hard ground.

The plane circled, banked for another strike. Lily held her breath, dug her nails into the dirt, watched the water spurt from the bag into a mud-soaked puddle.

The fighter dove again, the rancorous roar deafening them. A wing dipped, almost scraped the Jeep.

He's flying too low. So close I can touch it. If he's not careful...

The plane hit the ground, flinging sparks in every direction, skidding on its crumpled belly.

"My God," Lily said, watching flashes fly off the ground. "Flint and steel. My God."

Gideon gasped. "It's going to blow up. Got to get him out."

He scrambled out from under the Jeep, ran toward the plane.

"Get back. It's going to blow," Jalil called after him, but Gideon still ran toward the plane.

Jalil started toward him. "Gideon!"

The plane erupted with a whoosh and a deep rumble, exploding in a blast of fire and smoke. The hulk kept moving, momentum carrying it forward, black smoke and orange flames trailing in its wake. Gideon stood, arms stretched out, silhouetted by the bright raging inferno.

"Flint and steel." Lily crawled out, tried to steady her legs to stand.

"Flint and steel." She couldn't stop saying it, a formula for fire, for sparks of molten metal, for death in the bare desert.

"Fuel was in the wings," Jalil told her.

"Flint and steel," Lily chanted as the smell of gasoline and burning hair and flesh beat against her in waves of unbearable heat.

She stared at the blaze shimmering behind a haze of heat, the firestorm belching black clouds that billowed skyward, and horror chilled her skin.

"*Ma'a es salaam,*" Jalil murmured. "Go in peace."

Lily's legs wobbled; she could hardly stay on her feet. She crept toward the back of the Jeep, leaned her head against the doorpost, climbed inside, shoved the binoculars aside, and huddled against the seat.

She shook, tremors of shock disturbing the thick dust on the seat, her hands and fingers moving in circles. Her knees rattled and she clamped her hands between her knees to force them still.

She shivered as Jalil pulled Gideon back to the Jeep. "Hurry," he said. "Get in."

"We can't just leave him," Gideon said.

"Too late," Jalil told him. "Get in. Have to check the damage to H5."

"Back there," Jalil said as he drove toward H5 in a cloud of dust, "you were going to rescue the pilot before the plane blew up?"

Gideon nodded.

"Even though he tried to kill you minutes before?"

"He was a human being," Gideon said.

In the back seat, Lily, calmer now, unclasped her hands and gripped the side of the Jeep tenuously, bouncing with each jolt.

The fort guarding the pumping station at H5 was small, with irregular walls, built by the Desert Patrol. When the Jeep drew up, a soldier from the Desert Patrol emerged from a detached shed-like building.

"You all right?" Jalil called to the soldier.

"*Hamdulillah,*" he answered. "I took cover. Nothing I could do. Tried firing at them, but all I had was a rifle."

The soldier looked around and grunted. The walls of the fort were pockmarked, otherwise undamaged.

"No damage to the pipeline, the pumping station?" Jalil asked.

"No. I checked the gauges. I'll check again."

He turned back to Jalil before he disappeared into the shed. "The fighter pilot was not a good marksman," the soldier said, then added, "Not a good pilot either."

As he waited for the soldier's report, Jalil slapped his hand against his leg impatiently. "Have to get back to Azraq, have to radio Glubb."

The soldier emerged from the shed and told them that everything seemed to be in order.

"You'll be all right here?" Jalil asked him.

"*Inshallah,*" the soldier said. "I could use reinforcements, anti-aircraft guns. If the planes come back...." His voice trailed off and he shuddered.

"I'll check with Glubb." Jalil climbed into the passenger seat of the Jeep.

As Gideon started the engine and turned the Jeep, Jalil said, "We'll wait at Azraq for Glubb. Time we went to Tadmor."

Chapter Twenty

They sat outside, eating a Bedouin breakfast of fresh dates, Bedouin bread, and tea.

Hamud picked another date off the stem and squeezed it to pop out the sweet meat from the skin. "This is the food that is best. Did you know The Prophet himself broke his fast every morning with dates?"

The dates were delicious, sweet and succulent, and Lily kept eating, popping them with sticky fingers until her mouth was raw.

Hamud said to her, "You know, if you eat dates and drink water at the same meal, your stomach will explode."

"Seems reasonable." Gideon said as Lily backed away from the tray of dates and wiped her fingers on the towel in her lap.

And then Hamud told them that he had seen drawings of animals pecked into black basalt boulders in the Wadi Rajil. "All kinds if animals, animals with horns, animals with long necks. They have them there, in the Black Desert."

"We're here to do an archaeological survey of Trans-Jordan," Lily said.

Gideon nodded. "That's what they tell us."

"While we sit around waiting for Glubb, we could go to the Wadi Rajil."

Gideon nodded again and smiled.

◇◇◇

Gideon emerged from the fort carrying field glasses, a notebook, a 1-10,000 map of the Wadi Rajil area, with a pocket transit hung around his neck.

"That's all you're bringing?" Lily asked.

"This is a preliminary survey, just rough, to get our archaeological bearings. First we find a few sites. Then, we can go on from there."

"Where did you get the map?" Lily asked.

Gideon just looked at her. "You drive. Take the track east along that wadi. Hamud will tell you the way."

They set out along an eastward track, with Lily driving, Hamud in the back seat giving directions, Klaus aiming his camera at the sea of black boulders surrounding them, and Gideon leaning over the side of the Jeep to scan the surface. From time to time, he swept the horizon with the field glasses.

"This is how you do the survey?" Lily asked. "Just riding along the track?"

"Just drive," Gideon answered. "Do I sense a tone of disapproval?"

She nodded.

"If nothing has changed, the same routes were used in antiquity, so there'll be sites along here."

"But something has changed. There were volcanic eruptions."

"Some other time you can walk the desert inch by inch. For now, this is enough."

They rode further into the forlorn landscape of Wadi Rajil, skirting the basalt boulders that loomed across the track, with cinder cones all around them and black cliffs in the distance.

"Over there." Gideon lowered the field glasses and indicated a group of basalt slabs forty yards away, close to the edge of the wadi. "Crude images of gazelle and ibexes pecked into the rock surface.

Hamud pointed toward the slabs. "Strange animals. You see them?"

Lily veered in the direction of the petroglyphs. Klaus alit first, braced his camera against a steady boulder, and focused on the rock drawings.

Gideon picked up two small bladelets and rested them in the palm of his hand, fingered them thoughtfully. "There was water here once."

"Well, it's a wadi," Klaus said.

Gideon moved the basalt boulder aside. Underneath was a cache of small blades, geometric microliths, and bladelet cores.

"A knapping workshop." He looked up at Lily. "Epipaleolithic. Kebaran."

"Here? In the middle of nowhere?" Klaus asked.

"They were hunter-gatherers," Lily told him. "Moving all the time, following the food, just small bands, following gazelle and ibex, gathering grains. They didn't grow their own yet. They didn't even store it for the time of the year when food is scarce."

"When was this?" Klaus asked.

"Before the volcano erupted."

She wondered if the hunters cowered here when the volcano spewed fire, whether they fled in fear before inescapable lava, to be buried beneath it or to survive and have tales of the terrible day carried through time around magical campfires.

Suddenly, her stomach began to cramp, and her legs felt weak. She regretted eating too many dates.

"It was after the glacial maximum, but before agriculture," Gideon said.

He went back to the Jeep and pulled out some small drawstring canvas bags stamped with the words "Bank of Cincinnati," a British ordinance map, a prismatic compass, and a pocket transit from a box in the back and called to Lily. "Help me shoot this in."

"I can't." The cramp was more severe now, and she had to hurry. "Ask Klaus."

She grabbed her trowel and a roll of toilet paper from the Jeep and looked around for a place that would give her privacy. She spotted a small rise close to the cliffs and hurried toward it.

She was on the far side of the rise, just rebuttoning her jodhpurs when a mass of blue cloth enveloped her from behind, covered her head, wrapped around her arms. She struggled, and the cloth tightened.

She could hear Gideon's voice calling from a distance.

"Hello, Lily."

She tried to answer through the material pressed against her mouth.

The cloth tightened around her arms, around her chest.

Gideon called again.

"Hello, Lily."

The sound bounced off the cliff behind her, swirled against the boulders.

"Hello, Lily," echoed again.

She bent her leg and kicked backward, almost losing her balance. The impact reached up her heel through to her knee. For a moment, the cloth loosened. She managed to move her arm, reached for the trowel in her pocket, jabbed the cloth with it, and ripped open a slit.

Gideon called again, and now Hamud's voice was added,

"Hello, Lily. Lily. Lily," in ululations that rebounded all around her.

She slashed with the trowel, opened a tear in the cloth around her face, and saw the man with the straw colored hair, with his stainless steel knife poised, ready to strike.

She kicked again. Missed.

"Hello, Lily."

This time it was Klaus' voice.

Another echo? But the man turned. "Oh, it's you," he said to Klaus.

Lily lashed out once more, and Klaus twisted back the man's arm, wrested the knife from his hand.

Klaus stabbed the man in the chest, once, twice, and again. The man staggered, coughed, fell to his knees. Klaus stabbed him one more time before the man collapsed between two black boulders.

"Who is he?" Lily asked.

Klaus stood over him. "He was going to kill you."

"Do you know him?"

Klaus shoved the man tentatively with his foot. He didn't move.

"Next he would have killed Gideon. And after that…" Klaus turned away.

"Do you think he killed Qasim?" Lily asked.

"The others are waiting," Klaus said. "Time we went back to Azraq."

Chapter Twenty-one

From where she sat in the shade of the fortress, Lily watched Glubb arrive at Azraq in a homemade armored car: a Jeep wrapped in slabs of sheet metal. It caromed over the palmary near a pool of water where flocks of ducks drifted, argued, and dove for food.

Glubb parked the vehicle near the heavy basalt door of the fort. Awadh and Hamud emptied the Jeep. The car was loaded with more sheet metal for Gideon's Jeep, tins of food, two machine guns with mounts and magazine strips, three gelignite explosives with blasting caps, and what looked like an overnight case.

Glubb first showed Hamud how to hammer the sheet metal onto Gideon's Jeep to transform it to an armored car, and started him on it. Second, he grabbed the overnight case. Finally, he called Jalil inside.

Lily and Klaus followed.

The case contained a portable radio. Glubb showed Jalil how to operate it.

"I know how to work that," Lily said.

Glubb gave her a quizzical look. "You do?"

"If it's like the one we had in Tangier."

"This one is rather tricky." Glubb wrote down the frequencies for transmitting and receiving and handed them to Jalil.

All the while, Klaus watched carefully, focusing his camera on Glubb.

"What do you think you're doing?" Glubb asked him.

"Taking record shots."

"Records? For what?"

"My memoirs."

"You're writing a memoir?"

"When all this is over."

"Go away," Glubb told him.

Glubb closed the radio case and went back outside, where Hamud and Awadh sat in the shade.

All three, Lily, Jalil, and Klaus with his camera followed Glubb out.

"More record shots?" Glubb asked.

Klaus pointed the camera at him, "Say cheese," he said, snapped the shutter twice, stopped to reload, and started a new roll.

Glubb glared at him and turned away.

"It will take us at least a day to get things ready," Glubb said to Jalil.

He began working on the machine guns, aiming them at a target near a black basalt castle beyond the grove of palms.

Gideon came out. "Move the target. Have a little respect for history," he told him. "The foundation of that building dates to Diocletian. The upper portion is from the Crusades."

Grumbling, Glubb moved the target a few feet.

"We have to figure this out by trial and error." He squatted on the ground next to the guns, unable to conceal his disappointment.

"They gave us Hotchkiss machine guns from World War One, not the new Brens. These are not much good and nobody knows how to use them."

"I know the gun," Awadh scurried toward Glubb. "Lawrence used these."

"You were with Lawrence?" Glubb asked.

Awadh flashed a proud smile. "At Aqaba."

For a moment Lily saw a strong young fighter instead of the old man she knew, who sang tuneless songs to keep away djinns.

Glubb lifted one of the Hotchkiss guns and, fumbling, placed it on the bipolar mount.

"*Laa, Laa,*" Awadh told him. "Not that way."

He sat down next to Glubb, showed him how to set it up, then tried to load a magazine strip, bungled, and tried again. After an hour, with both of them working, the guns were assembled, loaded, and ready to go.

Two at a time, the men practiced firing, lying on the ground and aiming at the target, stirring birds that fled, flapping and calling, out of the palm trees behind them.

"Six of us." Glubb spoke over the incessant chattering of gunshots. "That's enough for a raid."

"Seven," Lily said.

Glubb looked at her. "Seven?" He shook his head. "There is no place for…."

Gideon eyed Lily. He raised an eyebrow, smiled, and then said, "Seven."

"I'm not sure," Glubb said.

"Seven," Gideon repeated.

"We'll see." Glubb waved a hand toward one of the machine guns and said to Lily, "Let's see what you can do."

She lay down on her stomach the way the others had, and pulled back on the trigger.

The recoil was more than she expected, and she reared back with a jolt.

A bird dropped out of the sky and landed in the pond amid a mutiny of startled ducks.

"You're aiming a little high," Jalil told her. "Have to correct that before we leave."

◇◇◇

Lily, Gideon, and Jalil breakfasted outside in the cool of the morning, escaping the airless heat inside the fort. Glubb had brought rolls, cucumbers, and tinned kippers, and it felt like a feast.

A man on a camel appeared over the hill, approaching slowly, with calm dignity. When he reached them, he slid off the camel and couched it. An embroidered vest covered his long white cotton galabeyah. A knife in a silver scabbard hung around his waist from a thick scarlet cord.

He gave a formal bow, "*Salaam aleikum,*" he said to Jalil with a flourish.

Jalil replied, "*Wa aleikum es salaam,*" almost automatically, without changing his quizzical expression.

"This is a formal occasion," Gideon murmured to Lily as the Bedouin and Jalil exchanged more greetings in Arabic, "*Sabach al kheer, Sabach al nur,*" wishing each other a bright, shining morning.

When Lily turned to go back inside the fort, Gideon stopped her. "Don't leave. I think this concerns you."

Closer, Lily saw that the Bedouin's knife hilt and scabbard were made of tin; his galabeyah was frayed at the hem, the black cloth of his vest had faded to a dark greenish gray.

The Bedouin told Jalil he was a Howeitat named Mahmoud ibn Nazeem.

"*Ahalein wa Sahalein,*" Gideon said. "Welcome."

Ibn Nazeem bowed again, looked over at Gideon, and addressed Jalil.

Jalil listened and turned to Gideon. "He is speaking for a friend."

"He is speaking for a friend," Gideon said to Lily, and ibn Nazeem spoke again.

"His friend has been watching," Jalil relayed to Gideon. "Your sister is very strong."

Gideon turned to Lily. "His friend has been watching you, and you are very strong."

Lily felt her face flush.

The Bedouin nodded and spoke again.

"He says she will make a good wife," Jalil said to Gideon, and Gideon repeated it to Lily.

"His friend will pay a bride-price of two camels and a donkey," Jalil said.

"No goat?" Lily asked.

"That's a very good price. They must think a lot of you." Gideon turned to Jalil. "No goat?" and Jalil transmitted the question to ibn Nazeem.

The Howeitat nodded and held up two fingers. "T'nane."

"Two goats," Jalil said.

Lily took a deep breath. "But how will I finish my dissertation?"

"Tell him," Gideon said, "that the offer is good. But I must warn him that she has a terrible temper."

Jalil passed on the message and continued with wide gestures, looking as if he was giving instance after instance of her appalling disposition.

"*Shukran,*" ibn Nazeem said to Gideon, thanking him. He bowed again, gave Jalil a heartfelt speech, took his leave, went back to his camel, untied its feet, and mounted.

"He's grateful that you were so honest," Jalil told Gideon.

"Am I really that bad?" Lily asked as they watched the Howeitat disappear over the ridge.

Gideon shrugged, and then smiled at her.

"It doesn't matter," she said. "They couldn't have paid the bride-price anyway. You saw how poor he was."

"And even if they could," said Gideon, "what would I do with two goats?"

Chapter Twenty-two

Beyond Azraq and the Wadi Sirhan lies a basalt wasteland; beyond that, the flat gravel desert known as hamad; beyond that, to the east, Iraq, and to the north, Syria and the Great Syrian Desert. That was the way they headed, toward Palmyra and T3, two armored Jeeps bumping along in a cloud of dust with Awadh following, proud, on his horse. Glubb Pasha drove the lead car.

They had started at first light, before the sun was hot. But by late morning, the desert heat and the added humidity in the enclosed space inside the Jeeps made the ride unbearable.

Lily's head pounded as she rode along in the second Jeep, boxed in by steel plates that reflected the sun. Water didn't help much. Neither did the roiling dust that covered the windshield, kicked up by Glubb's Jeep.

Gideon had tied a kerchief across his forehead to catch perspiration before it blocked his vision, but the sweat still poured down his temples and over his cheeks. In the back, Klaus sat with his eyes closed, almost comatose—his face red, his hands slack, his mouth open.

They had to stop twice, to sit outside in the shade of the Jeeps, wetting scarves they draped over their heads, and waiting for Awadh to catch up. For lunch, they ate cucumbers and watermelon, too exhausted from the heat for anything else, until Glubb insisted on handing out pickles. For the salt, he said.

"Only a hundred fifty miles to Palmyra from H3," Glubb said by way of encouragement. His uniform was wilting. "A hundred fifty miles to a pipeline that leads through Syria." He dabbed at his forehead with a linen handkerchief. "We'll make it handily in one day."

They stopped once more after they crossed the border to Syria, parking the Jeeps in the shadow of a wadi.

"Syrians aren't too bright," Jalil said. "You know what they say about Syrians?" He tipped his canteen over his kafiya to wet it and cooling water poured down onto his face. "When a Syrian goes into the desert, he always carries a door with him, so that when he gets too hot he can open the door and catch a breeze."

They reached Tadmor by late afternoon, when the air was lighter and the bright desert sun sat large and low on the horizon.

They parked out of sight in a low declivity, and stood outside the Jeeps for a moment, stretching, taking deep breathes of the dry, clear air. Waiting for Awadh, Glubb directed Hamud and Jalil to unload the gear from the Jeep. At last, Awadh came galloping toward them, brandishing his rifle, his cloak flying behind him.

Awadh alit and patted the rump of Ghalib, his horse, lovingly. The horse whinnied.

"For God sake, shut up that horse," Glubb said. "And keep low."

"I will try. But my horse is like a handful of wind, too swift to grasp, and the song he sings is in Allah's hands."

Glubb took in an impatient breath. "Just keep him quiet."

Awadh squatted on the ground next to the horse.

"You know how to handle gelignite?" Glubb asked him.

"I was with Lawrence from the Hejaz to Damascus."

"Along the railway?"

Awadh gave him a broad smile.

"Can you take care of the pipeline?"

He nodded before opening the packet that Glubb handed him. "Only three blasting caps?"

"That's all they gave us." Glubb shrugged.

Lily had brought the training rifle. Just as she had seen Bedouin do, she slung it over her shoulder with the strap across her chest.

They unloaded the Jeeps, and at a signal from Glubb, silently, they clambered up the slope, setting the gear down as they climbed, edging up to it, then moving ahead again.

As they reached the top of the ridge, Glubb whispered, "Keep low."

Gideon gazed across the two hills jutting out above the plain. "Palmyra. After the Romans discovered the course of the monsoons Palmyra replaced Petra as the entrepot for trade with China and India."

He squinted into the sun. Before them, nestled at the foot of desert hills, lay the remains of once magnificent Palmyra. "It was wealthy, elegant, a prosperous city that commanded trade routes that linked Persia to the Mediterranean." He gestured toward the remains of the city: a great colonnade with monumental arches, a theatre, a Temple of Baal, and, at the top of a hill, a medieval Arab castle. Scattered across the dusty plain, some tower tombs were still haunted by the souls of the dead.

"Underneath those hills lies ancient Tadmor. Silks and pearls, perfume and jewels once came through here," Gideon said. "And now look." Beyond historic Palmyra lay the collection of hovels that was modern Tadmor.

"And now, oil passes through here," Glubb said, "on its way to the Axis."

Glubb nodded to Jalil and Hamud. "The building on the hill on the right is the Foreign Legion outpost."

He indicated a small square building surrounded by pillboxes, the whole compound enclosed in barbed wire.

Jalil and Hamud started toward it in crablike movements, staying close to the ground.

When they had cut the barbed wire and shimmied through, Glubb and Awadh began to set up the Hotchkiss guns.

Gideon started down toward what looked like a trench near where they waited. "You coming?" he said to Lily.

"What do you think you're doing?" Glubb asked.

Inside the trench, a staircase led down to an elaborate carved door.

Gideon held out his hand toward Lily. "It's a hypogeum, an underground tomb," he said, and Awadh began to sing in his strange toneless monotone, just as he had in the Siq at Petra.

Glubb silenced him with a stare.

"They found it when they were digging for the pipeline," Gideon said

Lily had heard of it, the Tomb of the Shattered Pillar. It was not as famous as the Tomb of the Three Brothers, or those in the Valley of the Tombs, but it was part of the necropolis. Thoughts of the darkness of a tomb, to be trapped in the bowels of the earth and never return, chilled her.

"I can't go in there," she said.

"Why not?

"Who knows?" She tried to laugh it off. "Maybe there's a demonic ghula waiting inside. Maybe the hill could collapse and you and I and the Shattered Pillar, whatever it is, will be entombed together for eternity."

She couldn't muster a laugh that didn't sound nervous.

"And maybe," Gideon said, "You're afraid of what happened the last two times you were in a cave."

"This is no time for archaeological foolery," Glubb said.

Lily bristled. "Foolery? These are some of the most important tombs of antiquity, famous for their frescoes and sculptures."

"We're here to take care of the pipeline," Glubb said.

Gideon held out his hand to help Lily down. She couldn't move, and her heart was pounding. What was wrong with her?

"We have to do a clean job and get out," Glubb said.

Gideon stared at Lily and dropped his hand.

"Could be hidden armaments down there," he said to Glubb.

"Of course there could. This is a military installation." Glubb looked toward the Jeep. "We might have enough gelignite with us, but not enough blasting caps."

Gideon looked astonished. "You want to blow up the tomb?"

"Isn't that what you had in mind?"

"Not at all." Gideon clambered out of the trench. "Not at all."

Jalil emerged from the outpost, with Hamud following. "Seven of them."

"All inside the outpost?" Glubb asked him.

"That's all we saw."

"Did they see you?"

"I don't think so. But it may be too late. I think they spotted us coming and radioed Damascus."

Chapter Twenty-three

Quickly, Glubb and Jalil mounted the Hotchkiss guns on small tripods and attached ammunition belts.

Glubb gestured to the others, whispered, "Get into the trench and stay low."

With the guns in place, he and Jalil crouched down behind them, and waited.

They didn't wait long. Three soldiers came out of the fort, rifles cocked, aiming at Glubb and Jalil, and behind them three more, aiming at the others huddled in the trench.

Jalil and Glubb opened fire. Lily watched them fan the guns on their mounts, raking the discharge back and forth. Blood erupted from the soldiers' chests. Still, their legs kept moving until they fell, screaming, calling out. She felt dizzy and began to tremble, adrift in a miasma of the smell of cordite, bodies churning from the impact of shots, cries of the wounded.

"Oh God." Lily scrunched her eyes closed and held her hands over her ears while the guns chattered ceaselessly, rifles cracking, machines guns blasting, halting, starting up again, kicking dust.

"Oh God, oh God."

"One more, he's coming out now," Jalil said, and the Hotchkiss guns exploded again.

"That's seven," Glubb said into the sudden quiet. "You sure that's all?"

Lily opened her eyes and stared beyond the barbed wire fence, littered with blood and silent bodies splayed over the ground.

Jalil nodded. "Seven. That's the lot of them."

Glubb, his sidearm in hand, strolled over toward the fort, clambered through the hole in the barbed wire, and one by one, he inspected each bundle of mute khaki.

He fired once at one of the bodies. "Poor bugger," he said, and went on to the next.

Behind Lily, in the trench, the door of the Tomb of the Shattered Pillar, still on its ancient hinges, scraped open.

Ibrahim emerged from the tomb.

"We've been waiting for you, expected you yesterday." He leveled a rifle at those in the trench just as the buzz of approaching aircraft sounded in the distance.

Chapter Twenty-four

They scrambled out of the trench. Ibrahim followed, aiming his rifle at one, then at another, as they scattered across the flat desert floor. All except Awadh, who hid the gelignite and blasting caps in a corner of the trench, then went after his horse.

The hum of aircraft grew louder. Two fighter planes cleared the line of low cliffs at the southwestern fringe of the oasis, firing as they came.

In the open field, Lily and the others were perfect targets. They sprinted across, making for the trench at the entrance to the Tomb of the Shattered Pillar, with Lily and Awadh trailing.

Ibrahim looked up at the planes and waved, smirking, watched the men skitter across the dusty plain, then turned to where Lily stood next to Awadh and his horse.

"Now they're in for it." He raised his rifle again and pointed it at Lily. "And so are you."

The fighters, two hundred feet above the ground, dipped, roared down, fired at the Jeeps, climbed, banked away, and swooped again to fire another burst, shattering rocks into chips and flakes with a stream of bullets.

The aircraft tore overhead, engines roaring, machine guns spraying the area, whipping the ground into clouds of dust, coming in lower and lower, missing the trench where the others were huddled. Lily watched one fighter bank, fly toward the setting sun, fire at the ground.

"Can't see us," Lily heard Glubb say. "Sun in his eyes."

Lily lifted her rifle and leveled it at Ibrahim. He swung around and aimed his gun straight at her.

She pulled the trigger, felt the kick. A cloud of dust and rock shatter burst on the plain below, then nothing.

The gun fell from her hand. Ibrahim was ready to fire. Lily plunged to the ground, hitting her arm against the Hotchkiss tripod.

The barrel was still hot. She jerked her hand away as if bitten, then grabbed the trigger end of the gun, figured the magazine belt held at least twenty cartridges. She swung the barrel around, pointed at Ibrahim, pulled the trigger.

The recoil threw her back; the battery of explosions deafened her. She had missed Ibrahim.

But the plane behind Ibrahim erupted in a blast of fire.

She watched the fireball fall. The roar and crash of the plane, the sharp odor of gunpowder, gasoline, burning flesh hurtled against her, as if she were struck by lightening.

What have I done?

Ibrahim grabbed for Awadh's horse and pulled himself up into the saddle. He kicked the horse. It didn't move. He struck it with the butt of his rifle, pulled the reins to the left and right, struck the animal again with his rifle. It still didn't move. It whinnied and its ears laid back in rage.

Gusts of heat pushed against Lily. Flaming bits of fuselage dropped like leaves from the blooming inferno that hovered over the desert floor.

"May God consign him to hell fire," Glubb said.

Ibrahim cursed, kicked, beat the horse with the reins, the butt of his rifle. The Arabian shied, lifted its forelegs into the air, took off toward the Tomb of the Shattered Pillar, tossed its head back to unseat the rider. The stallion lost its footing, tumbled into the trench. Neck awry, the horse collapsed, coughed, shuddered, and died. Ibrahim lay on the ground, trapped beneath the horse.

Awadh scurried down into the trench, rifle ready.

He shot Ibrahim point-blank in the chest and looked up at Jalil.

"He killed my horse," he said, and shot Ibrahim again, this time in the head. "He killed my horse."

The drone of the second plane drowned out his voice. It had banked and ran at them again, strafing as it came, the path of the tracers angled toward them, churning clouds of dust along its path.

Awadh shook his fist at the plane and raised his rifle. He threw off his cloak, climbed to the top of the ridge and began firing at the aircraft, shouting at the plane. His kafiya swept away in the wind as the fighter banked and returned lower and lower.

"Get down," Glubb called, but Awadh kept shooting, aiming at the sky with a rifle.

The fighter dipped, fired a new volley, hit Awadh in his leg, his chest, his head, before it took off eastward toward Baghdad.

Awadh went down without a sound.

Hamud ran up the slope and Jalil followed. Tearfully, Hamud cradled Awadh's lifeless body, rocking him back and forth.

"Sometime, we all must die," Jalil said gently.

"He was a good, kind man," Hamud said. "And a hero in his day."

"If life were eternal," Jalil told him, "The Prophet would still be alive."

From below, Klaus looked at them. "In a war, people die." His voice cracked. "Both the good and the bad."

And Lily wondered why a pompous fool like Klaus had suddenly become sentimental.

They buried Awadh in a hastily dug grave next to the horse, hurrying to finish before the light faded, left Ibrahim lying where he had fallen, and prepared to go back south across the border.

Gideon lingered. "We can't leave Ibrahim like that."

"Don't worry, the Ruwalla will find him and bury him." Jalil said.

"How will they find him?" Lily asked.

Jalil pointed to a kettle of vultures, circling high above. "They'll show the way."

Lily shuddered.

"Carrion is carrion," Glubb said with distaste. "He wasn't one of ours. The Ruwalla can take care of their own."

"And the others, the ones from the Outpost?" she asked.

"Vichy French," Glubb said. "The fortunes of war."

Glubb retrieved the gelignite and blasting caps from the trench and signaled Jalil to come with him into the pumping station.

"Be ready to go," Glubb told the others. "We have only two minutes after I set the blasting caps."

Gideon and Lily brought up the Jeeps and kept the motors running while Klaus helped Hamud dismantle the Hotchkiss guns.

By the time Glubb and Jalil darted out of the pumping station, ducked under the barbed wire, and jumped into their waiting Jeep, Lily and Gideon had packed the equipment.

They took off.

At the sound of the explosion, Lily looked back. A fountain of debris filled with black smoke erupted from the pumping station. Flames licked at puddles of crude oil that seeped from the pipeline.

As they sped away into the twilight, the eastern sky was already dark.

Chapter Twenty-five

They camped that night on the side of a wadi. Glubb had brought along cans of bully beef and pineapple, and from somewhere, Jalil produced coffee ground with cardamom, sugar, cups, and a coffee pot. They had a decent dinner, sitting around the campfire, talking, winding down from the day.

"Back there at T3," Glubb told Lily, "You did a good job." He gave her an appreciative nod. "Shot down the plane. Very effective."

"It was nothing," she said, gazing modestly at the campfire. "I do it all the time."

"Shoot down planes?"

She gave him a mysterious smile and didn't tell him she was aiming at Ibrahim, even after Gideon raised an eyebrow at her.

Jalil pulled something from his pocket, a folding knife with a long blade and a stag handle.

"I found this at Wadi Rum when I went back to the site where Qasim was killed."

He opened the knife. Lily watched him run a finger along the top of the blade. A dark brown globule stained the corner of the blade where it folded into the handle.

"There's blood on it," she said.

Klaus shifted his leg and moved back from the fire. "Probably from some animal."

"Isn't that your knife?" Gideon asked, looking at him.

"No. I don't think so."

"It looks like it," Gideon said.

"It could belong to anyone." Klaus rubbed his hand across his mouth. "Anyway, I lost it. It fell out of my pocket sometime while I bounced along in the back of the *Gott verlassen* Jeep."

"When was that?" Gideon asked.

"I lost it at Jerash."

"You used it after that," Lily told him. "You used it when we were in Amman."

"I must have lost it in Amman."

"You used it after that," Gideon said. "In the Wadi Rum."

"Then I must have lost it in the Wadi Rum."

Indeed you did, thought Lily.

<><><>

Klaus had been silent through most of the dinner and lingered at the fire when the other men retired to talk and smoke and plan new strategies in the military tent that Glubb had brought.

Lily cleared the ground of rocks and pebbles and laid out her sleeping bag near the hearth. The fire had died down to a few orange embers and a wisp of smoke when Klaus began to speak.

"They arrested my son and my wife." He turned his head toward the remnants of the fire, and Lily thought she saw the glint of tears. "I've heard of terrible things, coming out of Germany."

Lily had heard rumors too.

Klaus turned his head toward her. "I don't believe those stories at all. Germany is the land of Beethoven and Goethe. I was born there."

Lily thought of the reports she had heard of officials so fiendish it seemed that a monster had devoured their souls.

"It's also the land of Wagner and Nietzsche," she said. Was it just propaganda, she wondered? What she had heard, tales of torture and brutality beyond the imagination couldn't be true. "And was once the land of Einstein and Thomas Mann," she added.

In the darkness, she could just make out Klaus' outline. He hung his head. "My son. My wife. Gone," he whispered. "They lied. They always lie."

"Who lied?'

"Gerta." His voice caught in a sob. "Gerta Kuntze. I suspected something was wrong from the very beginning, but now I know."

"You took orders from Gerta Kuntze?" Lily said.

His prolonged absences, his knife that Jalil found in Wadi Rum. It was all beginning to fall into place.

"You have to understand," Klaus said. "I had to work with her. Even though she is a Nazi. She told me that the life of my son and my wife depended on it. I believed her."

"So you weren't having an affair with Gerta."

Klaus bristled. "I'm a married man."

"And she was your Nazi contact."

An ember from the fire snapped. The spark glowed in the air for a moment before it vanished.

"I should have known all along," Klaus said. "Gerta would bring me letters that she said were from my wife, but the handwriting was different. Gerta said it was because my wife broke her arm and she had trouble writing with her arm in a cast."

He stared into the fire. "But in the latest letter I got, my wife called my son Johan. His name is Joachim. And she called me *Schatzi*. So now I know for sure."

"Who called you *Schatzi*?"

"My wife. She would never do that. She always called me *Leibling*."

"How did you get a letter?"

"From Ibrahim."

"Ibrahim gave you a letter from Gerta Kuntze? He worked for Gerta Kuntze too?"

Klaus wiped his eye with the back of his hand. "I should have known she lied. The postmarks of all the letters were wrong. We lived in Elberfeld, her parents were in Bavaria, but the letters were all mailed from Berlin. When I asked Gerta about it, it was always a different story. From that alone, I should have known she was lying."

"Like your stories about losing your knife?" Lily asked. She felt pity for him, and at the same time, anger—enough to confront him.

The light of the fire reflected a drop at the tip of his nose. Klaus wiped it off and sniffed.

"You killed Qasim," she said.

The words slipped out. *He could kill me now. The knife is in his pocket.*

Klaus turned and stared at her. His lips moved as if he was about to speak, but he said nothing. The fire flared and crackled as it died down.

"And I guess you slipped the scorpion into Hamud's robe," she said, careless with indignation, unable to stop.

"I had to." He spread out his hands. "Gerta told me to make sure your guide was someone who would report your plans to her."

His answer was calm, careful, as if it were rehearsed. Lily was revolted. "Have you no conscience?"

He waved his hands in a dismissive gesture. "Qasim and Hamud were only Bedouin."

You're no better than the Nazis, she thought. And said, "So was Ibrahim. You seemed sorry that he was dead."

"Ibrahim was a fool. These Bedouin," he swept his arm toward the desert. "They have wars of their own that we don't understand."

"And we have wars that they don't understand?"

He nodded and sighed. "They have no mercy."

He pulled up his knees, wrapped his arms around them, and began to rock back and forth.

"And the message for Gideon about the Rashidi. You overheard it?"

"It had to do with young Faisal, king of Iraq." He paused, took a deep breath, and looked toward the eastern horizon. "They plan to kill him."

"Who's they?'

"Gerta knows."

"And you. Do you know, too?"

"He's only eight-years-old," Klaus said. "Same age as my son."

For Klaus, a king might matter, but not a Bedouin.

The fire had died down. There was no moon and Lily couldn't see his face, but his voice was choked. "He's disappeared. I think Gerta has him."

"And the man from Wadi Rajil? You knew him."

Klaus turned away. "His name was Obersturmbannführer Dieter Erhard, a lieutenant colonel in the SS. He gave the orders to Gerta Kuntze."

"You have a conscience, don't you?" Lily asked.

"Of course I do."

"Then use it."

She climbed into her sleeping bag and turned her back to him.

If he's going to kill me, it will be now. Or in my sleep. I'll take my chances. I'm not a Bedouin. I'm a western, educated woman, and that matters to Klaus.

Maybe.

Besides, he saved me from the storm trooper in Wadi Rajil. That should count for something.

But her heart beat faster, and she had trouble falling asleep.

And in the morning, Klaus was gone.

Chapter Twenty-six

Hamud was already awake, sitting cross-legged by the campfire, tending the coffee pot, baking bread on a heated stone, preparing their breakfast of coffee, Bedouin bread, and dates.

No one seemed to miss Klaus, or seemed surprised that he was gone again, until over breakfast Lily filled them in about her conversation with Klaus the night before. She told them that he confessed to working for Gerta Kuntze.

And that he had killed Qasim.

Gideon held a piece of Bedouin bread in mid-air, halfway toward his mouth. Hamud, slurping his coffee, nodded over and over, as if it confirmed his suspicions.

"You confronted Klaus?" Gideon said at last. "Accused him of killing Qasim?"

"He admitted it."

"If someone kills once, they'll kill again. He could have murdered you, too."

"But he's gone." She leaned back, resting her hands in the ground behind her, remembering how angry she had been last night. "He said Qasim was only a Bedouin."

Hamud nodded again, this time more vigorously. "I knew he did it all along."

"How did you know?" Jalil asked. "You saw him?"

"*Laa,laa*. But he put the scorpion inside my galabiah."

"You knew that? Why didn't you tell us?" Gideon asked.

"You wouldn't have believed me." Hamud tossed his head to challenge him, and clicked his tongue against his teeth. "And what would you have done? He was one of you."

"One of us?"

"A *Franji* like you." He put down his cup and looked down, hiding the bitterness in his eyes, but not in his voice. "As you say, I am only a Bedouin."

"He told me that he was following orders," Lily said. "That he had to save his wife and son, that they lied. He was distraught, devastated." She looked over at Glubb. "He said there is a plan to kill young King Faisal, that it distressed him."

At the mention of the plan to kill Faisal, Glubb became as alert as a bird dog on point. When Jalil leaned forward to say something, Glubb put an impatient hand on his arm to silence him.

"What did he say about the plan to kill the king?" Glubb asked.

"He said his son is the same age as Faisal," Lily said.

Glubb waved her answer away. "What else did he say? This is important."

"Only that Gerta Kuntze has a hand in it somehow."

Glubb rubbed his hand across his chin, concentrating. "There's a rumor that Rashid Ali has been seen in Syria."

"Syria?" Gideon asked. "Not Iraq?"

"That's what bothers me. He knows that if he kills young Faisal outright, the country will be thrown into chaos. If he gets rid of the Hashemite regime, he'll get nothing. Sunni and Shiite religious factions will be at each other's throats. Rashid Ali is cunning. He won't risk that. He'll think of a better way."

"Is it more than just an Iraqi matter?" Gideon said. "Iraq isn't in the war."

"We need oil for the war effort. If he takes over, he'll block the pipeline through Trans-Jordan to Haifa. All Iraq's resources will go to the Axis."

"We have plenty of oil," Lily said. "From Texas, and California."

"That has to be shipped to the European Theatre by convoy. Ties up ships and personnel. And oil. And half the time, the convoy doesn't make it. U-boats are still on the prowl."

"Is that the reason Faisal is in danger?" Lily asked. "What do you think Rashid Ali will do?"

Glubb shook his head. "He wants power. He staged a coup once, last year. Ended in turmoil. We had to go in to establish order."

Jalil gave him a sardonic smile. "That wasn't the only reason you went in."

"Maybe not. But it was a damn good excuse. Rashid Ali doesn't want to give us that opportunity again." Glubb turned to Lily and spread out his hands. "You want to know what I think will happen? Young Faisal will disappear. Rashid Ali will probably kill him, but he'll use his propaganda machine to spread the rumor that Faisal's uncle, the regent Abd al Ilah, is responsible. Rashid Ali will arrive in Iraq to save the day, kill al Ilah, and take over."

He wiped his hands against each other, Arab style, to indicate a fait accompli, and Lily gave a shudder.

"Have to get back to Amman," Glubb said.

After a hasty end to their breakfast, they returned to Azraq by midmorning. As soon as they unloaded the Jeeps, Glubb left for Amman, and Jalil went inside to radio news of their successful raid at Tadmor.

When Jalil emerged from the fort, he looked worried.

"What is it?" Lily asked.

"Young Faisal has been kidnapped."

Chapter Twenty-seven

"Kidnapped?" Lily thought of the sad-eyed child with the sweet smile. King or no king, he was just a frightened child, and in danger.

"He was gone when his uncle went to wake him this morning," Jalil said. "There were signs of a struggle. A torn bed-sheet and some overturned chairs."

Gideon raised an eyebrow. "Seems feisty for a child."

"They could have used the bed-sheet to bundle him up," Lily said.

Jalil nodded "And deliver him to Rashid Ali in Syria."

"If Glubb is right," Lily said. "We have to find Faisal before they hand him over to Rashid Ali." She looked over at Jalil. "Klaus knows what's going to happen. He knows where they're taking Faisal."

"It's a big desert out there." Gideon waved his arm toward the stark desert expanse. "First, we have to find Klaus. All we know is he's somewhere east of here."

"The Bedu have eyes that penetrate the hills." Jalil squinted at the eastern horizon. "Some one has seen him. There are oases. There are wadis. There's even the Euphrates."

"So we go from camp to camp, looking for him?" Gideon asked.

"No time for that," Jalil said. "We must find Faisal before Rashid Ali gets to him. Otherwise, it's too late."

Lily tried to recall last night's conversation with Klaus. "Klaus told me he knew that Faisal was in danger from Gerta Kuntze. I don't know what else Klaus knows, what she told him." What else had Klaus said? There was something else about Gerta Kuntze. She couldn't remember. "I think he went to look for her."

It was Glubb, not Klaus, who said something about Gerta. In Amman. She remembered watching the fountain in the rose garden outside, Glubb speaking. She remembered young Hussein following them, and then she remembered what Glubb had said.

"What do you know about the Rashidi?" she asked Jalil.

"Their territory is east of here. They move back and forth across the Euphrates at the Ramadi Bridge, into and out of Iraq. Pasturage, not national boundaries, decide where the Bedu move."

"Do they have enemies?"

Jalil lifted his hands, palms up. "Only horses and hedgehogs don't have enemies."

"Gerta Kuntze lives among the Rashidi."

Jalil's eyes widened. "They range back and forth across the Iraqi border," he said. "If anyone could spirit Faisal out of Iraq, it's the Rashidi." He tapped his thigh, shifted his foot, looked east again. "If they still have him."

He turned to Hamud. "You stay here. Monitor the radio. You know how to get in touch?"

"With a radio?" He clicked his tongue, shook his head no. "You can show me?"

"*Inshallah.* Come inside."

While Jalil was busy with Hamud, Lily and Gideon reloaded the Jeep with fresh supplies: tinned food, extra ammo, water for their canteens. Gideon was filling the canvas water bag when Jalil emerged from the fort, this time carrying the suitcase with the portable radio, the field glasses, and the training rifle.

Smiling, he handed the rifle to Lily. "Your weapon."

She put it on the floor of the front seat while they hastily stowed the rest of the supplies and climbed into the Jeep.

"Somewhere east of here," Gideon commented as he started the motor. "All we can do is go east."

◇◇◇

They raced eastward along the road to H5, jarred from their seats as they bumped over dips and rocks in their path. Jalil sat in the back of the Jeep, sporadically surveying the horizon with field glasses. When they passed the place where they had gone off the road to the cave of Ibrahim's dog, he signaled Gideon.

"Over there," he said. "The cave with Ibrahim's dog. Someone's been there. See for yourself." He passed the field glasses forward. "I replaced the stone at the entrance myself. It's been pulled away."

"I don't have to look." Gideon veered off the road and bounced the Jeep toward the cave. "I believe you."

◇◇◇

They stood on the hillside watching the swarms of flies buzzing around the entrance to the cave, attracted by the smell of rot, the smell of blood that emanated from inside.

"I can't go in there," Lily said.

This was more than Ibrahim's dog, and that was bad enough.

"Neither can I," Gideon looked relieved. "Opening too narrow for me. Can't get my shoulders through."

Jalil gave him a scathing look. "Someone has to." He unstrapped his bandolier. "I'll try."

A few moments later, Jalil pulled out of the cave and moved toward the Jeep. He flicked a maggot off his right hand and wiped his hand on his cloak. He sat cross-legged on the ground, staring straight ahead, leaned over and retched. In his left hand, he held a watch. He rinsed his mouth with water from his canteen, wet the end of his *kafiya* and wiped his face.

He sat silently, catching his breath, swabbed off the watch with his damp *kafiya* and handed it to Lily.

"It's Klaus," he said.

Lily cupped the Schafhausen in her hand. The watch crystal was smashed, but the second hand still marched on, slower now, clicking forward, hesitating, clicking forward again, each time slower, winding down like Klaus' life. Last night, Klaus wept for his wife and child. And now, none of them is left, and there was no one to weep for Klaus.

"He bought the watch in Switzerland," she said.

"His camera?" Gideon asked.

"Smashed."

"How was he killed?"

Jalil looked up at him. "Difficult to tell. It must have been…" He nodded his head, rocked back and forth with his hands on his knees. "During the night some time. Time enough for the creatures of the desert to be at him. From what's left, it looks like his throat was cut." He wiped his face again with the wet end of his *kafiya*. "His gold tooth is missing."

Lily nodded.

"Gone."

"He was looking for Gerta Kuntze," Lily said. "Looks like he found her."

"But where is she now?" Gideon asked.

"Somewhere in Syria?" Jalil said. "Holding Faisal?"

Somewhere in Syria, Lily thought. Something nagged at her, something she couldn't quite remember.

She looked down at the Schafhausen. The second hand had stopped.

Chapter Twenty-eight

"There is an oasis near the Jebel Druze," Hamud said the next morning. "Near enough to Damascus, but hidden and secret. If they hide Faisal, it could be there."

"We can try it," Gideon rubbed his face and blew out his cheeks. "Nothing to lose."

"Nothing but time," Jalil said.

They loaded up the Jeep and left, going north past the pipeline road and passing the border into Syria before noon.

They drove along faint tracks through a bleak Syrian countryside scattered with forbidding black lava cones, past Druze villages where woman in colorful garb stood gossiping in the streets, past fields worked by black-robed Druze with white turbans who saw them and looked away. The grim black massif of Jebel Druze hovered over them. They skirted east of it, coming at last to a dark plain beside a fetid overgrown waterhole.

Two camels stood hobbled on the plain. And perched on the shadowy cliff above them, black and foreboding, stood the remains of a castle, walled and turreted, with tumbling basalt ashlars.

"A castle of the Assassins," Hamud said in a choked whisper, as if afraid of awakening their ghosts. "Even the great Salah edh Din feared them."

He rumbled on in an anxious murmur, his hand on the hilt of the dagger at his belt. "Anyone who tried to take an Assassin castle was dead before nightfall. Anyone who spent the night there would have his throat cut before morning." He took a tentative step forward, gripping the dagger. "Drunk on hashish and avarice. They killed or they were killed. Never captured."

He moved forward again, and began a cautious climb up along the fallen stones of the castle. Jalil and Gideon followed. Lily clambered after them, searching for footholds, clutching the edges of rocks.

They finally reached an archway and the remains of a vaulted tunnel and moved inside, along a debris-strewn passage reeking with the stench of animal dung and stale urine.

The tunnel opened out into a roofless room filled with rubble. Matted hair plastered against his face, a grimy Bedouin dressed in rags and a greasy sheepskin cloak sat in the center of the room leaning against a fallen rock.

Hamud took a step back. "He's from Ahl al Jebal, the people of the mountain."

The grimy Bedouin reached for his rifle, aimed at Hamud, shouted "*Wesh entum*? What tribe are you?"

Before Hamud could answer, the Bedouin fired point-blank. Hamud staggered backward. Silently, he dropped to the ground. His eyes, still wide with astonishment, had turned dull.

Jalil fired back. "He killed Hamud," Jalil said, and fired again. "He killed him."

Blood seeped from the grimy Bedouin's mouth, his nose. He collapsed onto the pavement and his riffle clattered on the stones.

Lily felt the color drain from her face, moved unsteadily toward Hamud's body. Gideon bent down to feel for his pulse, looked up at Lily and Jalil and shook his head.

"We'll take him back," he said. "Bury him in the military cemetery at Azraq."

"You think they're holding Faisal here?" Lily asked in a hoarse monotone.

Jalil looked down at the dead Bedouin, rolled him over with his foot. "Not these people."

"For ransom?"

Gideon stood up. "No harm in looking. You go that way," he said to Jalil, indicating the turreted area. "Lily and I will look there." He pointed toward what might have been the castle keep, its walls with courses still standing and reaching upward toward barrel ceilings.

Lily and Gideon set out into the maze of ruins. They found nothing but trash and tumbles of broken basalt blocks in weed-grown room after room, and over all, the reek of mildew and animal waste.

Once they heard a rifle shot, then another. They paused and looked at each other. "Jalil," Gideon said, and they kept going.

They found Jalil approaching them from inside a long corridor, carrying Hamud over his shoulder, fireman style.

"No one here," he said. "Just the two Ahl al Jebel." He shifted Hamud on his shoulder. "I took care of the other one." He moved forward again. "Let's get back."

They climbed down to the Jeep carefully, Gideon and Jalil carrying Hamud between them, Lily sliding down part of the way across the larger tumble of basalt blocks. Jalil carried Hamud to the back of the Jeep and covered him with the tarp.

Gideon started the motor and they drove over the basalt field, past the hobbled camels that brayed in their wake, back toward Azraq. Jalil looked back at the castle, craning his neck until it was out of sight.

""Ahl Al Jebel, the people of the mountain," Jalil said from the back seat. "They raid and steal and are against every man, every tribe, but mostly the Beni Sakhr. They killed Hamud." He lowered his head, ran his hand back and forth on the tarp. "He's dead and we lost another day. Lost, without finding Faisal."

"Hamud survived the scorpion's bite, to live a little while longer," Lily said.

"You see," Jalil said and shook his head. "There is no escape from what Allah has decided. And what has Allah decided for Faisal?"

Was that also the way with Qasim, Lily wondered, with Klaus? Was there no escape from the fate that Allah has decided? Even for Ibrahim?

The thought of Ibrahim made her shudder. She remembered Palmyra, remembered Ibrahim emerging from the tomb, remembered the plane that inexplicably took off for Baghdad, not Damascus.

"I know where they are hiding Faisal," she said.

Chapter Twenty-nine

While Jalil waited outside, pacing back and forth next to the Jeep, Gideon arranged for Hamud's burial, answering the objections of officers stationed at Azraq, arguing that Hamud had died in their service.

"Finally," Jalil said when Gideon emerged from the fort, and they set out, squinting into the morning sun.

They bounced along the pipeline road, through the basalt wasteland, until they reached the pumping station at H3, forty-five miles from the Iraqi frontier. They turned north and drove toward the mountains into Syria, through the Badia, the Great Syrian Desert, flat and treeless and blowing with dust.

They saw the palm groves and the mountaintop castle of Palmyra first, appearing in the distance like a magical mirage, and sped toward it, the motor groaning as they sprang over ruts and bumped across the rocky terrain.

Closer to Palmyra, Gideon slowed, and parked in the declivity where they had parked the last time.

"Palmyra again," Lily murmured, and shivered involuntarily. Everything had changed since she saw it last.

She stared at the ruins of the pumping station: a tumble of burnt rock, crazed and baked brick-red from fire and smudged by smoke; jagged remnants of the broken pipeline; the ground, greasy and dark from burnt oil; a mound of ash where the horse had lain. And over all, the pervasive odor of gasoline and burning oil.

And, when the wind shifted, a whiff of burnt flesh and hair.

Into the silence, Gideon whispered, "I will make your cities a waste, will bring your sanctuaries into desolation, and I will not smell the savor of your sweet odors."

And Lily shivered again.

"Rashidi," Jalil said, pointing with his chin at some Bedouin on the ridge and climbed out of the Jeep, and reached for his rifle.

Four camels, couched and grunting, sat at the top of the ridge over the pile of ash where the Vichy soldiers had fallen. Nearby, two Bedouin were seated at a campfire sipping coffee. A third seemed to be sleeping, his head resting on a camel saddle.

Where had they found fuel for a campfire in this God-forsaken landscape? Ashes of the fallen horse, swirling above the ground in tiny eddies with the breeze, looked as if they had been picked through for bones, and Lily turned away.

At the sound of the motor, one of the Bedouin at the campfire had turned. His eyes widened at the sight of a member of the Desert Patrol from Trans-Jordan coming toward him.

He leveled his rifle at Jalil. The blasts from Jalil's and the Rashidi's weapons seemed to be simultaneous but Jalil must have fired first. Jalil's gunshot hit the Rashidi squarely in the head, but the Rashidi's caught Jalil in the leg. Jalil's knee buckled. He collapsed on the ground, straightened his right leg slowly, recovered his rifle, rolled over on his stomach, positioned himself to fire.

Gideon scurried from the Jeep, dashed toward Jalil. The other Bedouin at the campfire headed for Gideon, pulling a dagger from his belt as he ran.

Jalil fired again, this time at the Rashidi by the camel saddle who was reaching for his rifle. Jalil hit him squarely in the chest.

Gideon tangled with the Bedouin with the dagger at the top of the ridge near the trench.

No way for Jalil to get a clear shot of the Rashidi struggling with Gideon. Lily could see that. The Bedouin struck Gideon's arm, his thigh.

Churning with anger, Lily grabbed her training rifle, clambered out of the Jeep.

Blood spread across Gideon's sleeve, along his trouser. He thrashed, kicked, clutched the Bedouin. They fell into the trench together.

Gideon grunted, twisted away, lifted his forearm against the Bedouin's raised dagger as unutterable rage propelled Lily into the trench.

She held her rifle by the barrel, swung it like a baseball bat, hit the Bedouin, swung backhand, hit him again. His head ricocheted. Anger bubbling from her throat, she hit him again and again, heard a crack, and kept swinging. Blood poured from the Bedouin's nose, his cheek swelled, and she kept swinging until he crawled out of the trench, keening, and loped toward the camels.

Lily turned. Gerta Kuntze loomed in front of her, feral as a hyena with her thatch of red hair and speckled face, brandishing Klaus' knife.

Lily swung the rifle, hit Gerta once, hit her twice. Gerta grabbed the butt, pulled on it, jammed the barrel into Lily's chest, knocked her down.

She attacked Lily with the knife, hit her sleeve, her arm. Lily grabbed Gerta's hand, bent it back until the knife fell, kicked it away.

Lily heard Jalil shout from behind.

Gerta grasped Lily's hand, opened her mouth, snarled, and bit into Lily's wrist. Lily screamed, shoved Gerta away.

Gerta grabbed Lily's hair, yanked her head back and forth.

Jalil yelled, "Lily, out of the way."

Out of the way, how? Her neck hurt, her wrist was sore.

From behind her, Jalil shouted again, "Out of the way, Lily."

Lily braced herself, pulled up her knees, jammed her feet against Gerta's hips. She pushed outward with her feet, threw Gerta back toward the door of the tomb.

Jalil fired. Gerta's mouth opened in surprise, blood sprouted on her chest.

Jalil fired again. The scatter of Gerta's freckles stood out like wounds against a whitening face. A fountain of blood poured from her neck.

An artery? Jalil hit an artery?

He fired again, this time hit Gerta's forehead. Her eyes clouded over. The fountain of blood from her neck pulsed, faded, pulsed again, trickled, then stopped altogether.

Further along the ramp, Gideon stirred with a low groan.

"You all right?" Lily asked.

"I'm okay. Just can't get up."

She stood her gun upright, barrel down, next to Gideon for support. "Here, hold onto this."

He put one hand on the rifle butt. She bent down and he placed his other hand on her shoulder.

Her neck still hurt.

He pressed his arm against her shoulder as she rose slowly, ignoring the twinge in her neck, hoping to haul him upward. He stumbled, fell, flinched.

"This doesn't work," Gideon said.

She caught her breath and they tried again.

"You need help?" Jalil called.

"Go see to Jalil," Gideon said. "I'll figure something out."

Jalil sat up and tried to stand. "It's my leg."

She held out her arm to help him and wavered under the pressure of his weight as he brought himself upright and braced himself on his rifle.

She went back to the Jeep, drove it closer to Jalil and Gideon. By the time she brought it around, Gideon had managed to edge up the ramp.

Leaning on Lily, Jalil got into the back of the Jeep. Both helped Gideon as he struggled onto the running board, heaved himself into the back seat breathing hard with the effort.

He rested a moment. "Without Klaus and without Gerta," he said, his voice thin and halting, "we'll never know where Faisal is hidden."

"I'm not so sure." Lily looked back to where Gerta lay. "Gerta came out of the tomb."

So did Ibrahim, she remembered. She started down the ramp. Klaus' knife lay on the ground where she had kicked it. She bent down and picked it up, wiped it off on her sleeve, folded it, put it in her pocket, and went further down the ramp.

Eyes averted, Lily skirted Gerta's body splayed across the trench and continued down, down the flight of stairs that led to the Tomb of the Shattered Pillar. She reached the elaborate carved door and hesitated.

She tugged at the door. It took all her strength to drag it open.

She took a deep breath, and stepping carefully, she entered the darkness of the tomb.

Chapter Thirty

Lily went down into a fissure in the earth as deep as midnight, past sarcophagi on either side topped with headless reclining figures, and then deeper into the blackness. The air was heavy, fetid with mildew and the odor of neglect. In the dim light, she could make out remnants of portraits of dead men carved into living rock along the walls; faint remains of frescoes, pale and peeling—portraits and gods, columns and vines; and a beehive pattern on a vaulted ceiling.

She edged deeper still, into the bowels of the earth where time rumbles through eternity, and heard a stirring in the far corner. An animal? A cat? A rodent?

Deeper into the abyss, into the stillness. She distinguished a bundle of clothing on the far corner and kept going. Closer, she saw it was a child, eyes wild with fear, a gag wrapped around his mouth, hands and feet tied behind his back.

She took the knife from her pocket, and he jerked back, his eyes exploding with terror.

"It's all right." She crept closer. The child cowered. "It's all right."

She cut the ropes that tied his wrists and feet with Klaus' knife, and untied the gag. She massaged his wrists and ankles and helped him up.

Staggering, he stood and pulled himself to his full four feet.

"I am Faisal, the King of Iraq," he said, with an imperial thrust of his chin. "Take me to my mother."

She took his hand to lead him toward the light. They stepped into the outside air and moved up the steps to the ramp. Faisal cringed and tightened his grip on Lily's hand as they passed Gerta Kuntze's body, and he wiped his cheeks and nose with the edge of his sleeve. Lily found a clean handkerchief in a pocket and handed it to him.

He took it, dabbed at his eyes, swabbed his cheeks, blew his nose.

"Kings are not permitted to cry," he told her, and gave her back the handkerchief.

<>< ><>

They rode south toward the Trans-Jordan border, with Lily's right arm draped across Faisal in the passenger seat, to hold him in place when they hit a bump. She drove carefully, avoiding ruts in the road to prevent jarring Gideon and Jalil in the back of the Jeep, and glanced at Faisal occasionally to see if he was all right. Once, she handed him back the handkerchief. He blew his nose and Lily drove on.

"You're awfully quiet," Gideon said to her.

"I've been thinking." She put both hands on the wheel. "When we went to Palmyra with Glubb, it was the first time I saw people killed in a war." Her voice trailed off as she drove around a boulder in the road. "The machine gun raked human beings across the middle as if they were cardboard." She lifted both hands from the steering wheel, wiped her face. "Unfeeling. Anonymous. Detach along the dotted line. I was horrified."

"Baptism of fire. That's natural," Gideon said. "It happens to every one. Nothing to be ashamed of."

"But today was something to be ashamed of." She gripped the wheel with both hands. "When I struck that Bedouin, I couldn't stop." She hit a bump in the road, her arm shot across Faisal to keep him from bouncing and she heard Jalil and Gideon gasp in the back seat. "The worst of it was, I felt a bizarre exuberance. Exhilaration. And I kept battering him."

"That was your adrenaline working," Gideon said.

"Adrenaline?"

"Fight or flight hormone. A basic instinct. Keeps us alive."

"It's a part of me I don't want to know about."

"Today you were a hero," Jalil said.

Hero? Lily drove on, carefully skirting boulders and furrows in the road, unable to overcome the feeling of self-betrayal. Once, when she hit a rut she couldn't avoid, she heard Gideon moan.

She glanced in the rearview mirror.

"All right," he said. "You convinced me. This is no job for a girl like you." She hit another bump and, in the rearview mirror, saw Gideon wince and grow pale.

"But you do it so well," he said.

"You certainly are difficult to kill," she said to Gideon after a while.

Gideon shrugged. "It works for me." The wind blew his hair. He pushed it back from his forehead, tossed his head and grimaced. "I laugh at death."

"Hah," Jalil said.

They reached the border before dark. After they crossed into Trans-Jordan, Jalil reached for the portable case to radio Glubb.

"They're sending two helicopters," he told them. "They'll meet us at H3 along the pipeline."

And now, at H3, she could hear the faint beat of the helicopters roiling the air. She looked southeast, and saw two dots approaching from a distance, growing larger, churning little dust storms in their wake.

The specks came closer, looking like a strange species of giant mosquitoes, their blades whirling against a cloudless sky. They flew closer still, and Lily could make out the Trans-Jordan flag emblazoned on the body: black and white and green strips overlaid with a red triangle and white star.

The helicopters landed in a flurry of wind and dust and noise, whipping up the ground and sharp, black lava pebbles.

"And then God answered from out of the whirlwind," Gideon said. "And said, gird up thy loins now like a man." He tried to get out of the Jeep. Breathless, he turned to Lily. "You'll have to help me out of here."

She reached into the Jeep for him just as two members of the Desert Patrol emerged from one of the helicopters and began to lead Faisal toward it. He looked back at Lily, blinking away tears. She nodded. He continued toward the helicopter and scrambled inside, assisted by the two Desert Patrolmen.

They came back for Gideon.

"Kings are not permitted to cry," Lily said to no one in particular, and she turned to help Gideon from the Jeep.

"I can't," he said. "Can't move my leg."

The Desert Patrolmen lifted Gideon from the Jeep. Gideon suppressed a groan.

"We'll meet you in Azraq," he said after he caught his breath. "You know the way? Just follow the pipeline road to H5, then take the track to Azraq."

The pilot stood in the open door of the aircraft and maneuvered Gideon aboard. She went back for Jalil. Jalil limped along, hopping on one foot, one arm across Lily's shoulder, the other carrying the closed suitcase that held the radio. At the door of the helicopter, the pilot took the suitcase and helped Jalil inside.

She watched as they took off, one helicopter eastward toward Baghdad, the other westward toward Azraq, and then she started the Jeep.

Chapter Thirty-one

Lily sat in the visitor's chair next to Gideon's bed at the Hadassah Hospital on Mount Scopus. Gideon had insisted on being flown back to Jerusalem. Jalil had stayed behind in the military hospital at Azraq.

"A broken pelvis," Gideon told her. "Upper and lower pubic symphysis. The doctor said I'd have trouble giving birth if I get pregnant."

"You're planning on getting pregnant?"

"The doctor is a gynecologist. It's all he knows."

"Why a gynecologist?"

"They're short on orthopedic surgeons."

"I thought Jerusalem had a surplus of doctors."

"Most of the orthopedic surgeons joined the Jewish Brigade, and are off in the Western Desert."

"At el Alamein." Lily felt a twinge of sorrow remembering Rafi, looked down at her lap, clasped her hands, unclasped them, looked out the window toward the university across the road.

"Who do you suppose killed Klaus?" Gideon asked her.

"Probably the Rashidi," Lily said after a while. "Under orders from Gerta."

"What makes you say that?"

"They took his gold tooth, but left the Schafhausen, smashed the camera. A European would have done the opposite."

"And Gerta ended up with his knife."

"I took the film that he left to be developed," she said.

"And?"

She handed him the packets of photographs. "Mostly what he said it was. Desert vistas, rock drawings."

"And the rest?"

"Some forts, defenses, inside of some pumping stations. Some of Azraq."

He opened one of the packets and fanned through it. "Take them a while to train someone to replace Gerta and Klaus. We bought time, that's all." Gideon sighed and adjusted his legs under the blanket. "We bought time."

"Meanwhile, Faisal is safe a little while longer."

Gideon put the photos back in the envelope. "I'll look at them later."

"I heard from Glubb," Lily said. "Rashid Ali is back in Berlin."

Gideon shifted under the blankets again and sat up, leaning on his elbows. "At least we did that much."

◇◇◇

She sat in the chair by the window while Gideon dressed to leave the hospital. The young kibbuztnik in the next bed was in visible pain.

She had met him the day before when she visited Gideon.

His name was Moshe. He was a member of the Palmach force fighting in Syria, and had lost an eye. In spite of his visible pain, he flirted with her and exuded sexuality.

He had told her that archaeology was his hobby, that he had a collection he had gathered from archaeological sites, and she said that was looting, that artifacts out of context lose their meaning as voices of the past.

Moshe smiled at her and winced at the pain and told her she was beautiful.

Gideon had just limped back into the room, leaning on a cane. He was dressed and ready to leave.

"Watch out for Moshe. His hero is King David," Gideon said.

"He intends to conquer Judea?" Lily asked.

"And make love to all the women in it, just like David."

"One can only hope," Moshe said.

<> <> <>

Gideon stood outside the hospital while they waited for the taxi. He crossed over the road toward the university, and leaned on his cane.

He stood at the edge of the hill on Mount Scopus and looked down at Jerusalem, at the Old City enclosed in its ancient walls, at the Tower of David, at the new city growing around Jaffe road and reaching to the far horizon.

"It's all there," he said. "Jerusalem, thou art builded as a city, that is compact together."

He took a deep breath, sighed, then shambled back toward the hospital. Lily helped him into the taxi and they rode down the hill to the American School.

They ate dinner at the American Colony in the courtyard. Omar Jibrin, the cook, chief bottle washer, and majordomo of the American School had gone to spend the weekend with his family in Ein Karim.

Lily had ordered lentils and rice and chocolate gateau, specialties of the house. A journalist from the Associated Press from the next table over approached them.

"Just back from Trans-Jordan?" the man from the Associated Press said. "Maybe you could clarify something." He put both hands on their table, leaned down, and said in a confidential voice, "I heard a rumor that little Faisal, king of Iraq, was kidnapped."

Lily looked at him and inclined her head. "Let not your heart faint, neither fear ye for the rumor that shall be heard in the land."

Gideon gave her a sideways glance, a look of astonishment on his face. Then he smiled.

"It's from Jeremiah," she said.

Gideon nodded. "I know."

"What about it?" the journalist asked. "Was he kidnapped?"

"A rumor shall come one year," she said. "And after that in another year a rumor, and violence in the land, ruler against ruler."

Lily thought the meaning was obscure and the translation awkward, but the journalist seemed satisfied, smiled, said thanks, and went back to his table.

Lily was dumbfounded. "What did I say? That was from Jeremiah, too."

Gideon cocked an eyebrow once again. "I think you gave it all away."

Sukenik, an archaeologist from the Hebrew University, and his son, Yigal, came into the garden, nodded to Gideon and Lily, and sat down at the next table, and said "Shalom."

Gideon answered "*Shalom, shalom, ve ein shalom.* Peace, peace, there is no peace," and took another forkful of the chocolate gâteau.

Acknowledgements and Notes

Although much of the book is based on historical fact, I fudged on the date of Glubb's Syrian campaign, moving it up a year. The Allies were already in control of Syria when this book takes place.

Glubb Pasha is a real historic character, as are Emir Abdullah, and the children, Prince Hussein (later King Hussein of Jordan) and the child King Faisal II. There really was a plot to kill Faisal, and there really were raids on the pumping stations of the oil pipelines.

And, for that matter, there really were Nabateans. Their capital, Petra, has changed much since it became a tourist attraction after it was declared a World Heritage site and one of the new Seven Wonders of the World. I was there when Bedouin still lived in the caves. For an interesting take on some of the legends encouraged by tourist guides that have grown up around Petra, see an article, "Petra—Myth and Reality" written for the *Saudi Aramco World*, and now on the Web by Philip Hammond, one of Petra's excavators.

An archaeologist, Nelson Glueck, really did do a survey of Trans-Jordan for the OSS, and he really was on the cover of *Time* magazine. The media tried to make another Lawrence of Arabia out of him, but he would have none of that.

Most of the rest is fiction. The last name of Moshe, the young kibbutznik in the hospital who lost an eye in a raid in Syria is Dayan. He really did conquer Judea, and loot archaeological sites.

Yigal Sukenik, the son of archaeologist Eleazar Sukenik, who founded the Department of Archaeology at the Hebrew University, did exist. He studied archaeology under his father, and later changed his name to Yigal Yadin, the code name that he used when he was in the Hagganah.

After the war, in 1946, the Emirate of Trans-Jordan under the British Mandate became the Kingdom of Trans-Jordan and Emir Abdullah became King Abdullah I. Trans-Jordan became the Hashemite Kingdom of Jordan in 1949.

Prince Hussein and his cousin Faisal did go to Harrow. Hussein went on to Sandhurst, the prestigious British military academy equivalent to our own West Point. Faisal went back to Iraq to take up his duties as king and was murdered during a coup d'état at the age of nineteen, along with his uncle, Abd-al-Ilah, who had acted as his regent and advisor.

My thanks certainly go to the intrepid archaeologist, theologian, and university president, the master of archaeological surveys, friend of Bedouin and Kings, Nelson Glueck, who could spot a micro-blade no bigger than your fingernail from the back of a camel. His experience doing an archaeological survey of Trans-Jordan was the inspiration for this book, and he was the model for Gideon Weil. In his spare time, he was also President of Hebrew Union College, and spent numerous years as the Director of The American School of Archaeological Research in Jerusalem, now known as the Albright Institute. Although many of his pioneering conclusions have been modified by subsequent research, for those interested in further exploration of Glueck's work in Jordan, you might look into his publications: *Exploration in Eastern Palestine*, published in 4 volumes between 1934 and 1951 by the American School of Oriental Research, a scholarly presentation of his Trans-Jordan survey; *The Other side of the Jordan*, a popular account; and *Deities and Dolphins*, a popular work based on his excavations at Nabatean sites.

I have also used *The Story of the Arab Legion*, an account by Brigadier John Bagot Glubb, known as Glubb Pasha, who directed the Arab Legion and helped bring order and control to the chaos of independent warring tribes for the establishment of a peaceful government in Trans-Jordan, and the memoirs of King Abdullah of the Hashemite Kingdom of Jordan, published by the Philosophical society in 1950 as references.

Many thanks go to Jessica Kaye, literary lawyer and agent extraordinaire, to Cherie Skinner, Department of Entomology at the University of California, Riverside, to Donna Todd, Sandra Battista, Ann Van, Laurie Thomas, and Craig Strickland for numerous suggestions in the course of writing this book.

And my eternal gratitude goes to the indomitable Barbara Peters, to Annette Rogers, Robert Rosenwald, Jessica Tribble, Marilyn Pizzo, and the rest of the staff at Poisoned Pen Press, for their skill, encouragement, and patience.

—Aileen Baron.

To receive a free catalog of Poisoned Pen Press titles, please contact us in one of the following ways:

Phone: 1-800-421-3976
Facsimile: 1-480-949-1707
Email: info@poisonedpenpress.com
Website: www.poisonedpenpress.com

Poisoned Pen Press
6962 E. First Ave. Ste. 103
Scottsdale, AZ 85251